HART'S
DESTINY

HART'S DESTINY

Kimberly Adkins

Black Lyon Publishing, LLC

HART'S DESTINY
Copyright © 2012 by Kimberly Adkins

Our books may be ordered through your local bookstore or by visiting the publisher:

www.BlackLyonPublishing.com

Black Lyon Publishing, LLC
PO Box 567
Baker City, OR 97814

This is a work of fiction. All of the characters, names, events, organizations and conversations in this novel are either the products of the author's vivid imagination or are used in a fictitious way for the purposes of this story.

ISBN-10:   1-934912-43-3
ISBN-13:   978-1-934912-43-0
Library of Congress Control Number: 2012932893

Cover Model: Jason Aaron Baca

Published and printed in
the United States of America.

Black Lyon Paranormal Romance

This book is dedicated to Ellis White,
for his years of friendship, support and encouragement.
If only he could learn to use his powers for good …

Chapter 1

"You've only been back home a few weeks. I'm sure Emily wants you to come to the wedding. You can't expect people to know what you're doing these days if you don't tell them."

Jessica navigated the small parking lot carefully, hoping a spot would open so she could get her nagging companion out of the car. Her small-town friend was probably right, too. But that didn't mean she wanted to hear a lecture about it.

It was hard enough to admit the big life she planned after college wasn't going to pan out. Everyone thought she'd marry the head of the debate team, move to Washington, D.C. and guide her brilliant husband into a political career that would usher in a new era. Her golden-boy candidate might make it, but the constant press wasn't something Jessica was able to handle. Not after she discovered the parade of women who came and went when the lights were off.

"Jess, just get near the store and let me out. They close at five o'clock, ya know. I thought a big-city girl like you would have learned how to get a parking space by now."

She was shaken out of her reverie to discover that someone had easily cut her off for the spot she had been closing in on. "Sorry, Lucy. I'll get you close and then circle around to the back. After I park I'll meet you outside the store."

"Just come in. You have to pick up a wedding present, too, and I know what Emily wants."

"Yeah, maybe," she said.

Lucy unbuckled her safety belt and grabbed her coat before hurrying across the parking lot. She disappeared into the Christmas crowd on the sidewalk and pulled into one of the alleyways that ran behind the shops.

This time she was ready when a car began to back out of a space in the rear parking section. Jessica slammed on the gas pedal and her tires squealed in protest at the unexpected acceleration. The car shot forward to claim the spot when a small dog ran out in front of her bumper.

She hit the brakes with both feet and her heart pounded in her chest as inertia propelled the automobile deeper into the space. The tall figure of a man darted forward, so quickly that she could barely make out his features. He tucked the small dog under his arm and sprang away from her bumper as the car stalled out.

Jessica was shaking like a leaf as she tried to retrieve the keys from the ignition. The door creaked as she swung it open and stood next to the vehicle, gasping for air. She was light-headed and nauseated as she approached the man. He carefully put the raggedy dog on the ground next to a tree filled with white Christmas lights.

"Thank you. Oh my God, I don't know what I'd have done if you hadn't been there."

His back was to her while she spoke. She could hear him murmuring to the dog as the shivering bundle of fur appeared to settle down.

Her hero stood and turned slowly to face her. Though Jessica had regained her breath, she lost it again when she saw him fully. She felt like everything all around her slowed to a grinding halt and the air took on a heavy silence. He was at least a foot taller than her, and Jessica was not a short girl. He had a thick, full head of rich brown hair that spilled over the shoulders of his long leather coat. She could see his faded denim jeans underneath, and a pair of black motorcycle boots. He looked so out of place, like a rock star stranded in the middle of a corn field.

He stood stock still, watching her for what seemed like an eternity as she tried to make out his expression, though his dark sunglasses made it difficult.

She knew she should say thank you once more and be on her way. Maybe a polite nod would even do. But she couldn't make her feet move or tear her eyes away from the rugged, handsome man who saved the dog.

She brushed her unruly hair off her shoulders with a nervous gesture and resolved to turn away when he began to walk toward her. His movements were agile and graceful as he approached and she almost got the feeling he was trying not to startle her. He stopped a few yards from her and she could catch the scent of him on the cool breeze. He smelled like leather and musky spice.

She took a few steps forward and reached out her hand. She thought she might shake with him, but he never removed his hands from his pockets and she found herself placing her palm on his right forearm instead. The leather of his jacket was soft and supple from his body heat and made her realize she'd left her own coat in the car.

He didn't move when she touched him. All of a sudden she wanted to wrap her arms around him more than anything in the world. What harm could a friendly thank you hug do, anyway? Jessica closed the small distance between them and slid her arms around his waist, although she kept them on the outside of his coat. It was meant to be a quick gesture, but as she came up against his solid figure she impulsively laid her head on his chest instead. She knew she should pull away, that her actions were forward enough to be ridiculous, but she felt so comfortable that she relaxed against him.

The dark stranger allowed her to linger with his hands still safely tucked away for longer than she would have thought. When he finally stirred she knew he'd push her back and they could both go on about their business.

"Dammit," he growled low under his breath and the vibration of his deep tone rumbled through her entire body.

He freed his hands and she prepared to separate from him, but he slipped his arms around her instead and returned her hug as he held her against the length of his body.

Her sweater lifted off her back a few inches and exposed her skin to the cold, but his large hands covered the small of her back protectively as he leaned his head down and softly nuzzled her neck with his cheek.

A wild shiver flew through her body in response to his intimate action and he abruptly released her. Her legs were a little shaky and she nearly stumbled on the sidewalk as he took a few steps back.

Once he saw she'd regained her balance, he nodded behind his dark shades and disappeared into the alley behind them.

As Jessica turned in the direction he'd gone she noticed Lucy standing nearby, her jaw wide open.

"Who in the world was that?"

"You're not going to believe me, but I really have no idea," she said.

She felt a tap on her shoe and looked down to see the skinny brown dog wagging his tail as he tried to get as close to her leg as possible.

"Aren't you a cute little fellow!" Lucy bent down to pat the stray on his head before she straightened up to face her friend.

"Look, we can stand here all day and talk about how it would be cruel to leave this puppy out in the cold and how the poor guy looks half starved. Or, we could just pick him up and put him in the car because I know you're going to take him home anyway. Besides, it can't hurt to have a friend who doesn't think you're crazy."

"Is that what you think about me now?" Jessica asked, already imagining a spot in the apartment where the little guy could sleep.

"It's one of the things I love about you, I can say that," Lucy said.

Neither girl saw the mysterious stranger as he watched from the shadows of a nearby building, as still as a statue until they were gone from sight.

•

Jackson cursed to himself under his breath as he made his way through the holiday shoppers. The crowd didn't bother him much. Most of the people out and about instinctively shied away from his path without realizing it. He often wondered if something deep inside them sensed he was different. It was always this way when he mixed with a normal group, which is one of the reasons the woman he'd just encountered troubled him so much.

The last thing he needed at the moment was an attachment to a female, let alone one who wouldn't understand him or grasp his way of life. But he'd be damned if this one wasn't different somehow. He'd sensed her excitement and fearlessness when she wrapped her arms around him. He wanted to resist her. In fact, he couldn't remember a time when he'd lost control of his desires.

Her scent still clung to his clothing and skin. He absentmindedly rubbed the palm of his right hand against his cheek where he had taken the outrageous liberty with her before he came to his senses.

Stop it!

This was not a distraction he could afford right now. He was here on serious business and already walking a tenuous line. He had a responsibility he was going to see through and everything depended on it. Hell, everyone depended on it and he couldn't let his guard down for even a moment. Not for anyone he knew well and certainly not for some random young woman on the street.

He raised his palm to his cheek again and went on his way.

Chapter 2

"I never got an invitation, you know." Jessica did her best to reason with Lucy, who had decided beforehand they would come back to Jessica's apartment to wrap their gifts. "Don't you think it would be rude for me to show up at Emily's party the night before the wedding, too? What will she think? I'm crashing two buffets for the price of one?"

Jessica fumbled a little with the ribbon on her package. She truly had reservations about attending the wedding, let alone the bridal party's dinner on the evening before. She only picked up the present to pacify Lucy and the money she spent was well worth the hours of peace that followed. Besides, her friend could always take it along with her own.

"You act like we're going to a torture chamber for a night of horror," Lucy said. "Has it ever occurred to you maybe she wants to see you? Emily has been living in Seattle for as long as you've been on the East Coast. To be honest, even I haven't had the chance to catch up with her since she came back for the festivities, she's so busy. Nothing but text messages and phone calls! I'm dialing her right now and we'll clear this whole thing up. Besides, my friend, I don't have a date, so you're it."

"Well, just don't plan on a cheap one. Dinner and a movie isn't gonna get it, sister," Jessica teased as she finished with the package.

Lucy held up one finger as the phone rang. Jessica assumed she was about to explain their plight when a puzzled look came over her impulsive friend's face.

"Yes, I'm at her apartment, actually. That's why I'm calling you back. Wait ... okay. Let me put her on." Lucy walked across the living room and held out the cell phone with a shaky hand.

"She wants to talk to you."

There were more than a few questions on the tip of her tongue as she took the phone, but the sound of Emily crying on the other end stifled them all. "Listen but don't say anything, okay Jessica?" The voice on the other end sounded almost nothing like the level-headed friend she had known and loved so well through school.

She nodded and immediately felt ridiculous because Emily couldn't see her.

"Can you please come to my dinner tonight? I need someone to talk to, someone who might understand what's happening to me. I love Lucy, but she's never left home and doesn't know much about the outside world. I'm afraid, Jess. I don't know what to do and I think maybe this has all gone too far."

"Can you tell me what you mean?"

"I'll tell you when I see you," Emily said.

"I'll be right there."

•

The limousine arrived to pick the girls up less than an hour later. There were no markings on the town car, no company logos anywhere. While it was a nice touch to ensure the no one in the party intended to drink and drive, Jessica felt a little vulnerable in the backseat of the luxury sedan. She realized she didn't know where the car was taking them and it was a good bet Lucy didn't either.

"Are you sure Emily hasn't said anything strange to you on the phone since she's been home?" Jessica asked her friend quietly, watching the chauffeur's silhouette for any sign that he could hear her. She perused a well-stocked wet bar in the back, but didn't feel inclined to imbibe. Lucy held up a passing hand, a little more flighty than usual.

That's saying a lot, Jessica thought to herself as she regarded her old friend. If anyone saw the world through rose-colored glasses it was Lucy. It was quite possible that Emily did try to talk to her seriously, but to no avail.

"She might've mentioned a couple of things, you know. Jitters and stuff. Everybody who gets married has them, right?"

"That didn't concern you at all? And do you even know where we're going tonight?"

"Oh, yeah! Of course I know. Hold on a sec, I wrote it down somewhere," Lucy said as she dug threw her giant leather handbag, retrieving a dozen or more crumpled napkins with random phone numbers on them.

"Um, all those napkins and you can't get a date for the wedding?" Jessica snickered in the shadows of the limo and noticed they were well past the bright street lights of the town. The windows were tinted, but she could still make out a thick wall of trees alongside the steep road. It was too bad the moon was only half-full or she'd be able to see more.

"I could get a date, sure," she said, taking no offense. "But not everyone is good enough for this. We're talking about Emily, remember? Best friends forever and always?"

"I'm honored you chose me, then." Jessica returned her smile warmly, remembering their motto when they were younger. Just as she was beginning to feel better about the whole thing, Lucy pulled out the wedding invitation.

"Here it is. I wrote it on the back so I wouldn't forget."

She took the thick vellum envelope from her friend and was surprised by the weight of it. She turned it over and saw Lucy's erratic scrawl along the edge, but her attention was captured by the thick wax seal, which had been chipped and broken.

"Is this some kind of family crest in the wax? It seems so ancient and regal."

"You're asking me?" Lucy shrugged. "I didn't look at it too much. I think it's a claw or something and a flag, maybe a grail."

"You're such a sage. How could I ever have doubted your wisdom?"

"You think I have wisdom? How cool! Anyway, the directions are there."

Lucy pointed back to the edge of the envelope and Jessica did her best not to laugh as she read out loud. "Big castle out in the woods not very far from the city. Can't miss it, sending a car."

"This is what I'm talking about!" Lucy squealed in delight as the sedan slowed, and peered as best she could through her darkened window. They pulled onto a curved black marbled driveway laced with white veins. They couldn't even hear the vehicle idle as a uniformed man emerged from the walkway to open their door.

The frosty evening air rushed into the interior of the car and made the women eager to be on their way. Lucy thanked the valet with a flirty smile, but his handsome face showed no reaction as he closed the door behind them.

Gentle lights reflected off the mirror-like surface of the drive and Jessica turned beneath the courtesy awning to look out over the mountains. She could see the lights from their tiny town very far in the distance, but she had no idea where they were. She pivoted around to appraise the hillside above them and was stunned to see the sharp relief of stone turrets against the twilight sky.

A shiver that had nothing to do with the cold wind ran up her spine. If she hadn't known better, Jessica might have thought someone was watching her from the lofty parapets, but that would be paranoid.

"When did they build a castle in Hocking Hills? I've never seen anything but cabins and lodges around here and I grew up in this neighborhood," Jessica said as they followed the winding path toward the front.

"Who cares? This place is awesome!" Lucy said as she fished around in her leather bag and pulled out a tube of lipstick. "I can't wait to see Em. She must have really met a great man on the West Coast to get this sort of treatment. I hope there are some cute guys here tonight."

"Is that still all you ever think about?"

Lucy shrugged with a grin and expertly applied a deep red color to her lips. In a way, Jessica found it comforting that her friend hadn't changed much over the years. Lucy had always been the outgoing, popular type, whereas Jessica preferred to observe most things from a distance before she jumped in. It wasn't that she was anti-social, just a bit cautious. She really preferred to think of it as dependable.

And here she was, being dragged along by her friend to a fabulous party just like the old days. This was probably good for her and even if she wasn't sure about that, Emily needed her and that's what dependable friends were for.

The front doors were massive and lit by torchlight. The flames whipped inside their iron sconces and caused shadows to play across the intricately carved patterns on the doors. It was a weird effect that made it seem as if the sculptures were moving along the panels.

Before they could reach for the door knocker, the heavy planks opened with a creak. A man stepped from behind the opening and gestured for them to enter.

The foyer was warm and dimly lit, but the shadows barely concealed the beautiful furnishings that welcomed new visitors to the manor. A winding staircase curved along the right side of the hall. Exquisite portraits hung in gilded frames on the wall all the way to the top of the landing. Jessica thought the whole place looked like something out of a movie, not anything that could exist in the small, nearly Appalachian countryside where she'd grown up.

Another well-dressed young man joined the first and helped the girls out of their coats. There was a bit of an awkward struggle when Lucy refused to give up her hand bag, but her attendant backed off gracefully when she made it quite clear that wasn't going to happen.

Jessica easily gave her satin evening purse to the gentleman who took her coat and added a small thank you to make up for her companion's behavior. The pleasantry came out soft and quiet, like it would inside a museum or lecture hall.

What kind of party is this going to be? If there's a conservatory and a lead pipe I'm out of here! Just as the thought crossed her mind she noticed the lingering stare of the young man who held her things. His eyes were brilliantly blue and the corner of his mouth quirked up with a charming smile when she caught him looking.

Jessica blushed and was horrified that she should react to such a simple thing as a smile. Oh God, they'd probably think she really was a backwoods country girl. Still, he was strikingly handsome and she smiled back as he ran his hand through his dark blonde hair, doing his best to hide the grin that had taken over his face as he turned away.

Lucy was openly flirting with the one ushering them through the corridor that lay beyond the foyer, though she didn't get much of a reaction. He was polite and proper in every way, only turning to look over his shoulder at Jessica to make sure she was following them.

"Hey, do you have any other lipstick in your purse?" Jessica moved up to whisper in Lucy's ear. The last thing she had on her mind before they left was looking pretty at the party tonight, but she suddenly found she was conscious of her appearance.

"Are you kidding?" Lucy answered her in the same confidential tone. "Lancôme called me today and asked if they could have their makeup back. If red isn't your thing, I've got plenty more."

She pulled out several different cosmetic bags until she found the one that contained at least a dozen tubes of color and glosses. Jessica had barely gotten the lipstick on when they entered the dining room. She was glad she did, because she found herself in a room full of immaculately dressed strangers who looked more like they were heading to a royal coronation than a bridesmaid dinner. She felt pitifully underdressed in her simple black blouse and long skirt. The scrutinizing looks from the others in the room let her know they didn't miss a thing. The cold appraisal from the three other women in attendance came off as shrewd and disapproving.

"Do you think maybe you were wrong about the night of torture thing you mentioned earlier?" Jessica asked quietly as she leaned close to her friend

"It'll be fine. If they're Em's pals, they can't hate us. Besides, free drinks and cute guys everywhere, see?"

Jessica had to admit that everyone in the room was unusually beautiful or handsome, but it was more than that. They gave off an aura of grace with the way they held themselves, even in the way the women looked down their noses at them. She didn't know who the heck Emily was marrying this weekend.

She barely heard the shuffle from behind before she felt the polite touch on her elbow and turned. Her shoulders relaxed when she saw the blue-eyed stranger who helped her earlier at the door.

"You must be Jessica." He said her name like it was a special thing and the sound of it carried a little across the room.

"I could be Lucy," she said a bit playfully, seeing how well he had done his homework.

"You could be." He cast a glance over his shoulder to the red-haired girl surrounded by at least five men who hung on her every word. "But if you were, I'd certainly never have a chance to speak to you alone like this."

"I don't know about that." Her heart beat faster. This gorgeous guy could be over there with the rest of Lucy's fan club, but she felt almost certain that he had singled her out when they first arrived.

That never happened when she was out with her beautiful friend.

"Perhaps you would agree to sit next to me during dinner? I'd enjoy the opportunity to converse with you on a more personal level."

He's good looking and uses words he doesn't have to look up in the dictionary? This must be my lucky day!

Jessica nodded and allowed him to escort her to the table, where she was dismayed to find seating cards on the linen. Her name was obviously next to Lucy's and one of the other women she hadn't met yet.

"I guess that fate is against us," she said.

"Which is nonsense, of course," he replied. "I can control my own fate, at least for this last night."

Before she could ask him what he meant, he picked up the card to her left titled *Meredith* and flung it carelessly to the opposite side of the table. As he settled his own card down in its place, she noticed the name Roland written out in delicate calligraphy.

"I hardly think that's proper etiquette, do you?" The high-pitched voice was obviously agitated, but looking into the eyes of the woman who could only be Meredith it was difficult to discern her emotional state. Her skin was fair as porcelain, her hair so pale that it might have been white. If it hadn't been for her piercing green eyes, Jessica would have thought that she was an albino. Either way, she was stunning.

"I never have much say about what is proper, now do I?" Roland asked.

"Be that as it may, I should think you'd be more concerned about the reason your bride-to-be hasn't joined us for her rehearsal dinner than wooing one of her childhood chums."

The words hit Jessica like an icy slap to the face. Meredith couldn't have missed her reaction a mile away, though she had no look of triumph on her face. Instead she gazed sympathetically toward Jessica.

A sinking feeling filled the pit of her stomach. She was fervently thankful she hadn't had anything to eat or drink yet, because she was pretty sure it would have come directly up and onto the floor of the fancy dining hall.

Roland somehow managed to look angry and apologetic all at the same time, but he was clearly unable to explain. When the pale, stately woman rounded the table and took Jessica's arm, she allowed herself to be led away.

"Please accept my apology, young lady. This was an unfortunate event I did not anticipate. Emily is waiting in her room, unwilling to come down. Perhaps you could see her for a moment?'

"Can you blame her?" Jessica could hear that the tone of Meredith's voice was sincere but she was furious all the same. How was this any different than the situation she walked away from in D.C.? "I hope you don't expect me to try to change her mind. I can tell you right now that won't happen."

"I don't expect you to do anything but listen to her. I doubt you will understand, but at this point we hardly have anything to lose." Meredith steered her toward a doorway on the opposite side of the room from which she entered.

Jessica did her best to orient herself so she could get back to the foyer on her own if she needed to, but they were on a mountain, for God's sake. Even if she did find a way out, where would she go on foot?

And there was Lucy to consider. She was clearly having the time of her life and Meredith had done nothing to discourage that situation from developing. Maybe if she could see Emily, talk to her, everything would make sense.

Any attempt to keep her bearings was thwarted by the many stairwells and corridors they traversed, but Meredith did nothing to cause her any concern along the way. *Maybe that's because I'm willingly going where she wants me to.* Emily better be behind door number one or she's going to see just how good a country girl can survive.

Her doubt vanished when Jessica heard the exhausted cry of her friend before they were even in front of the bedroom door. Meredith politely knocked but got no response. After turning the knob and opening the door a crack, she motioned for Jessica to enter.

She didn't hesitate for a moment and stepped inside before Meredith had a chance to follow. Jessica closed the door and locked it behind her with a swift motion.

"Jess?" The familiar voice of her friend reached her ears and all the memories they shared together while growing up came back to her in a flash.

Emily sat up on the bed, eyes red-rimmed and voice rough. But it was truly her best friend in front of her and she chastised herself again for losing contact with one of the few people in the world she loved.

"I'm sorry, Emily. I'm so sorry I've missed all this time with you." Jessica threw her arms around the trembling girl and held her against her chest. "We have to get you away from here now. Lucy is in the dining room. We'll scoop her up on the way out and you can stay at my apartment."

Jessica knew that Emily didn't have anywhere else to go. Her parents had passed away years back and their house was long gone. She and Lucy were really the only family Emily had now.

"I can't leave, Jess."

For a moment she wasn't sure what she'd heard, but the fact that Emily remained firmly planted where she was let her know she meant what she said.

"Listen, I know this is hard to hear, but Roland doesn't deserve you. You should come away with me right now."

"It's true, Jess. Roland doesn't deserve me, but he's stuck with me."

"What do you mean?" Jessica was floored. "No one could ever be stuck with you. Marriage should be about love."

"You're right and I don't love Roland."

"Then why—"

"I'm not good enough to be with the man I love. They gave me to Roland. He did not choose me. They want me to mate with him and put my other feelings behind me."

"Mate with him? Do you have any idea how crazy this sounds?"

"Please, don't say that to me! You are the only one I can trust. Lucy couldn't grasp it at all. And this isn't Roland's fault, either. He was burdened with me."

"I won't pretend I understand, but we can work this out. Nothing is final yet. How about you come over to my apartment and stay for a while? The wedding isn't until this weekend. It will give you plenty of time to get your feelings sorted out."

"You always were the most level-headed one of us." Emily smiled through her tears and it warmed her heart to hear the girl say it. It meant she was listening. "Go along to dinner like everything is fine and tell them I'll be down in a bit. I'll pack a case and have the driver take me over tonight, so don't worry if you don't see me before then."

"If you're sure that's the best way to do this, but I really think you should leave with me now," Jessica said.

"In case you hadn't noticed, though I'm not sure how you'd miss it, there are a lot of politics and family ties involved. I'll smooth things over and come right to your house. I promise."

"I'll be up all night until you get there," Jessica added, and knew she would probably get very little sleep even after her friend arrived. With her fingers on the doorknob she nodded one last time to the girl in the room and slipped into the hall.

The carpeting was thick so her footfalls didn't make a sound as she mentally retraced her steps. She was so focused on her thoughts that she didn't see the figure lurking at the end of the corridor before the top of the stairs.

"Did Emily tell you the truth?" Roland's voice was low and surly. She suspected he'd had a few too many glasses of wine in the interim and the haphazard way he held his empty crystal goblet confirmed as much.

"She told me enough," Jessica said. "But this is not a conversation you and I need to be having."

"So you know there is no love between us."

"I know she doesn't love you," Jessica hammered out the words with no hesitation and he visibly flinched as they hit home.

"Her heart already belonged to another man, far more powerful than I am. Neither one of us can be blamed for that."

Roland advanced but she held her ground, unwilling to show any sign of temerity. His eyes almost glowed when she refused to back down, though it appeared to increase his ardor.

"Who's this person she's interested in, then?"

"It shouldn't matter to you, my lovely girl." He pitched forward slightly on the pretense of intoxication, but Jessica was wise.

"I strongly suggest that you don't touch me," she firmly bit out the words as he came forward again, but in the blink of an eye he had her pinned against the wall. Her head was spinning—she hadn't seen his movements. Both her arms were locked by her side against the rough wallpaper. She knew she was helpless but it would be a cold day in hell when she panicked in front of any man who thought he could take advantage of her.

"I won't hurt you, sweet girl. Just one kiss from a man to the woman he admires."

Jessica's muscles were stiff and she forced herself to relax so she could make her move when the time was right. In her opinion, the time was right before he managed to kiss her. She slipped the heel of her right foot up and rested it against the wall.

For a brief moment she thought she saw movement in the alcove directly opposite of their location. The shadows were dark and impenetrable so she couldn't be sure, but she sensed they weren't alone. That feeling was confirmed when light flashed off two eyes in the depth of the recess and a deep, threatening growl issued from the alcove.

Roland froze and a rush of palpable terror washed over his face. Before she could move he released her wrists and turned to face the sound.

"My Lord," Roland murmured and fell to one knee on the posh carpet. In a bizarre gesture he tilted his head to one side as if he was deferring rank.

The darkness gathered shape and a figure came together as a man emerged from the passage. Jessica was stunned when she recognized him, not in his leather and jeans, but in a full dinner suit—the gorgeous man from the shopping mall.

"This little dalliance is nothing, My Lord." Roland's voice was full of shaky assurance. "I still follow your will, as in all things."

"I think not." The tall, formidable man spoke clearly in front of her for the first time. Ever since their encounter at the plaza Jessica had imagined what his voice sounded like outside of a frustrated growl. Now she knew, even though he was angry, his voice was beautiful.

Roland looked at her in panic, just briefly, before he turned back to the dominant man in the doorway. "Are you saying you disapprove of this situation?" he asked.

"You're not a foolish man after all," the tall man answered him again in the most even-keeled, civil tone she had ever heard.

Roland's eyes grew wide with sudden comprehension.

"Please forgive my actions; I did not know she was yours!"

"Now you do."

The statement was flat and merciless. Roland skittered off like a whipped dog into the distance.

Chapter 3

What was she doing in his family's home?

Jackson's heart thudded in his chest so violently that the others in the vicinity must have sensed his emotion during the challenge. And make no mistake about it; he would have challenged Roland to a terminal fight over the woman who stood frozen in the hallway before him.

She was breathtakingly lovely, possibly even more so because she didn't know it. By God, she must be so frightened, so confused—but strength radiated off her curvaceous figure like a light he could nearly bask in. This woman was ready to fight for herself and her friends with no guarantee she would prevail, he was sure of it.

I knew I should have turned away the moment I saw her beautiful face.

This was ridiculous. Fate just didn't cross the mighty Jackson Hart on his untouchable throne at the head of the family lineage. Yet here she was, standing before him a second time. He had a terrible feeling this slip of a girl was going to complicate things for him greatly.

"What did Roland mean when he said that I was yours? You'd better explain what's going on here and what you've done to Emily, or I swear I'll call the police and tell them you're holding her against her will."

Such strength in the face of a dangerous adversary! Her determination and loyalty tore away at the barrier he kept so tightly around his heart. It was everything Jackson could do to keep himself from pulling the dark-haired spitfire into his arms and exploring her passionate nature further. His blood pumped through his veins, driving his instinct, but he was forced to admit there were serious concerns at present regarding Emily. The one thing he wanted to do more than anything in the world would be his undoing if he followed his desire right now. As always, he must put his duty first.

"He meant, of course, that you are my guest this evening." He carefully leveled his tone. "This is my house, after all, and I assume you are here to dine with us."

"I'm here for Emily, not you, My Lord." Her voice was sharp. *Damn, the woman doesn't miss a thing.*

He knew he had to get her into the dining hall with the rest of the others before people could talk, but a part of him was unwilling to let go of even the small amount of time he had alone with her. Even if she was angry, she was there with him and wasn't afraid. It had been a long while since he found himself with a woman who had no idea who he was.

"Perhaps I may offer to escort you back to the table? I'm sure everyone will be waiting for you."

The look on her face softened as her shoulders relaxed. She stood away from the wall and appeared to consider moving closer to him in the corridor.

"Look, you've been nothing but kind to me, especially after everything that happened earlier today. Let's start again." She completely closed the distance between them and held out her hand in the same way she had earlier that afternoon. "My name is Jessica. I really hope you're someone I can depend on."

Her hazel eyes were beautiful and full of striking color when she looked up at him. Jackson couldn't resist the opportunity to touch her, and he smoothly grazed her wrist with his fingertips. He knew the clan would talk now. He knew they would be right, too. Her scent was all over him, intermingled with his own pheromones. At the moment, none of that mattered next to her hand placed in the palm of his.

"I just want to get Lucy and go home, if it's all the same to you. I don't think Emily will be coming down to dinner, but please promise me that she's free to leave if she wants to. I'll be waiting for her."

Jackson nodded to her wishes. She smiled a little awkwardly and looked down at their hands, and it spurred him into immediate action as he used his hold to fold her right arm inside his left. He had offered to escort her and it would be properly done.

Perhaps it was best for Jessica and her friend to leave before more intrigue could disturb the clan. This whole business with the wedding had his family in an uproar as it was without this little surprise thrown in. If he had known the drama that was going to be involved with a trip back to Emily's hometown for these nuptials, he never would have consented to her one wish.

And then you would not have met the lovely woman at your side, said the angel sitting on his right shoulder.

Precisely, the devil responded.

Besides, he had a feeling he was far more unsettled by her than anyone else at the party, at least for the moment. Jackson told himself she would be safer elsewhere—he just wasn't willing to admit maybe she'd be the safest from him.

•

Jessica wasn't able to stretch out on the couch with her furry little roommate curled at her feet, but at the moment she was thankful for a little warmth and comfort. The dog she'd named Scruffy was at the most twenty pounds soaking wet, but she still felt safer with the pup.

It wasn't as if he'd been keeping her up anyway. She was far from sleep with all the thoughts in her head from their little dinner party debacle earlier. She kept replaying the events in her mind, and lingered on the moments spent with Jackson most of all. He never actually told her his name as he led her back through the winding corridors. Somehow the silence had been perfect. As wonderful as her arm felt against his, she understood any words could break the spell—the same way she knew on the cold sidewalk earlier in the day that being with him was right.

The moment they'd entered the dining hall she could have heard a pin drop. Her little bubble was instantly burst as a dozen or so sharp gazes landed on them.

Lucy's laugh carried across the room from her place at the table, and though it wasn't any louder than usual, the unexpected sound cut the silence. Even her friend had the decency to blush at the startled looks from the people around her.

That's when she heard Meredith say his name. Jackson. The woman was between them before she could blink and the next thing she knew, she and Lucy were being shown the way out. It took some convincing on the ride home before her friend believed they weren't ejected because of anything she'd done, but once she learned that Roland was the groom-to-be, she was as equally incensed as Jessica. All they could do was wait for Emily to come if she could.

Lucy slept fitfully on Jessica's bed, neither girl wanting to separate. Jessica would have had no trouble joining her, but the couch held a most excellent view of the front door and she watched it constantly for any sign of Emily's arrival.

Jessica grew drowsy despite her resolve. She pulled a small blanket off the back of the couch to tuck around the sleeping dog that shivered from time to time at her feet. She took up the slack and pulled the rest of the cover over her hips and as far as it would go around her waist. No harm in being warm while she waited, was there? Her eyelids grew heavy and she found herself blinking in an effort to focus on the white lacquered door. She was just about to nod off when the click of the lock permeated the haze and she sat bolt upright on the couch.

Emily must have remembered their old trick from childhood, leaving a spare key on the door frame up top in case one of them needed to get inside. Jessica was never able to shake the habit and in truth, it came in handy more than once when she found herself locked out of her home as a responsible adult, too.

Scruffy sprang from the couch and ran to the opening door. Jessica called to him in case it wasn't Emily, but he didn't listen. His tail wagged and he looked very happy to greet the newcomer.

The door swung open the rest of the way and for a minute she was blinded by the glare of the porch light. A large shadow entered through the frame, much too large to be Emily.

Her fierce guard dog ran up to the figure as he emerged into the front room, but instead of showing any signs of hostility, Scruffy sat promptly and began to lick the uninvited guest's outstretched hand.

As her eyes adjusted to the light she recognized the man behind the shadows. Jackson stood in the middle of the room, looking at her with his deep brown eyes. "I knew you had brought him home, of course." He smiled at her and the approval in his voice washed over her like a soft caress.

"How did you find me? Us, I mean. Did Emily tell you where I was?"

"My driver picked you up and brought you back, Jessica. Remember?" His answer was simple, yet the way he spoke her name sent a delicious shiver up her spine.

"Is Emily with you?"

"I didn't come here to talk about Emily or about Roland, or even Lucy. I am here for you." He came closer. She caught his distinctive scent again, the aroma from his skin and clothing that made her a little dizzy every time.

"I don't understand what you mean. Why did you come here for me?"

"Let me show you, beautiful girl."

Jackson was immediately in front of her. He was just an inch away from touching her and that small amount of distance was torturous. She wanted more than anything to feel him against her again—the way things had been when they met and everything seemed right.

"When you offered me your hand this evening, I wanted to take more. I came here tonight because I couldn't stop thinking of you. Because I couldn't stop thinking of touching you."

He took her fingers up in his large hands and began to gently push the black fabric of her blouse away from her wrist. His thumb pressed underneath the cuff, feeling her pulse before he slid his fingers along the delicate skin of her inner arm. His touch was like fire against her body and she raised her arm in his grasp, snaking it around his neck and allowing the rough, dark stubble from his jaw to scrape.

He ran his lips along the pulse point of her neck, grazing her with his teeth. He growled again, his tone deeply passionate as he gently bit her. It felt amazing at first, but his amorous vocalization began to sound almost feral, dangerous. His kiss grew sharp, painful, as she tried to pull away.

Darkness covered her eyes and she panicked as she understood she was suddenly alone. When she reached out for Jackson she began falling backward through the floor into a vast nothingness. The warning bark of a dog reached her ears in the void and she truly sat straight up this time, gasping for air as she touched her unscathed neck.

Oh, God. I was dreaming! She looked for Scruffy, who stood his ground between his owner and the sleek silhouette in the doorway of the now opened door.

Emily held her own in the porch light, not advancing but unwilling to retreat.

Jessica shivered when she saw her friend's face, her teeth bared in defiance at the dog that stood between them. For a single second, she wasn't sure who was more dangerous.

Chapter 4

"What's going on, you guys?"

Jessica was temporarily blinded when Lucy flipped the switch of the overhead light in the living room. When her eyes adjusted she had to cover her mouth to keep from laughing out loud at her disheveled friend. Lucy had rifled through the storage drawer in her dresser and chosen a pair of tube socks and an oversized T-shirt that read *WHAM!* across the front.

"Hey, if I spend the night, too, can I get a Duran Duran shirt?" Emily said from the doorway, and all three women dissolved into childish laughter.

Whatever tension had hung about the room a few minutes before was gone with the darkness and they were the best of friends again, getting ready for a slumber party. The new puppy even relaxed a little and came back to sit at her feet.

"I really missed you." Lucy clung to Emily, who returned her embrace. "Jess took off to the East Coast and you went to Seattle. I was so lonely for a while, but now I know that someone had to stay home so you guys had a place to come back to!"

"And I'm glad of it, for sure," Jessica said as she watched Scruffy approach the newcomer.

"Don't worry about this little fellow." Lucy knelt down to pet the young dog. "He's new, but he's super nice once you get to know him."

Scruffy rolled over on his back and allowed himself a belly rub from the girl to the chorus of "Who's a puppy? You are!" But when Emily reached out to give him a pat, he stood up and retreated to his spot next to Jessica.

"We'll all know a lot more about what's going on now. Right, Em?" Jessica asked pointedly, trying to draw her friend's attention away from the dog.

"Sure. I'm going to tell you everything that's been happening just as soon as I get a little rest. I'm exhausted."

Emily looked beautiful standing in the middle of her living room, dressed to the nines for the bridal party. There was an underlying look of weariness behind her eyes, and Jessica noticed her covert glance toward Lucy.

"Oh, good," Lucy said with relief. "I was really tired but I didn't want to miss anything. We can talk over breakfast in the morning. I'll make pancakes!"

"Sounds great." Jessica smiled with genuine feeling. It was an old high school tradition of theirs, pancakes made by Lucy. Mostly because she couldn't cook anything else to save her life. "I'll just get Emily settled in and we'll all chat when we get up in the morning." Miss WHAM 1984 gave a tired wave of her hand and disappeared into the bedroom. The two remaining women didn't move until they heard her plop down onto the bed and gently begin to snore.

"Somehow it's comforting to see Lucy is still the same person she was back in school," Emily whispered as she crossed the carpeted room in her high heels to gently shut the door of the bedroom.

"You know, I thought exactly the same thing. In a way, she's fared a lot better than we have by staying here."

"I have a strange feeling you could drop her off in the middle of the Brazilian rainforest and she'd be queen of the natives in no time, teaching them how to do Jell-O shots while playing Spin the Bottle."

"Everyone likes Lucy, even tonight at your party. There were half a dozen fine looking gentlemen paying her lots of attention." Jessica tried to sound nonchalant, but she wanted to ask her friend more about those unusual people they had met at the manor house. Deep in her heart she wanted to find out about Jackson, but didn't know how to go about it without seeming too interested.

"Who was paying attention to her?" Emily abruptly asked with sharpness to her words. There was a definite tone of jealously in her voice, which caught Jessica off guard.

"Oh man, Emily. I didn't really know who anybody was tonight." Jessica walked into the kitchen and fumbled around in one of the drawers for a wine bottle opener. A glass of wine might help Emily relax.

Emily approached the counter that separated the kitchen from the living room and took a seat on one of the bar stools with a sigh. "I'm so sorry about all of this, Jess. My emotions are everywhere and you wouldn't believe the layers of politics that go on with the Hart clan. I never know who I can trust."

"So, Roland's last name is Hart?"

"It's a little difficult to explain to someone who hasn't been around the family. It's the Hart bloodline, but only those with a pure vein of it carry that surname. Roland is half-blood. He's actually a Ceridian."

Jessica poured the wine into each of their glasses and the sweet fragrance of the Otter Creek Traminette filled the air. "You've always been a strong girl. Out of all of us I thought you'd be the one who'd rule the world—or at least a small island somewhere with summer apples and a wicker man. This seems like a patriarchic-dominated group of people. I never thought you'd buy into that sort of thing."

"Then it should be obvious to you that it would take a magnificent, strong man to impress me." Emily's smile showed in her eyes and Jessica could see her warm reflection.

Her heart beat faster with her friend's words and she knew she was right. Just the memory of her two encounters with Jackson—yes, she could easily see why this family inspired such devotion.

"Tell me about him then." Jessica felt closer to her friend than she had during the many years of their brief and sporadic online communications.

"I'll gladly do so if you hand me that glass of wine."

Jessica took a long sip of her own smooth vintage as she passed the bulbous glass across the counter.

"He's amazing, Jess. He's just so …" Emily wrapped her hand securely around Jessica's wrist and yanked half her body over the counter with a strength Jessica found surprising. "You've been with Jackson, haven't you?" Her voice had dropped so low it was a mere rumble.

"Been with in what way?" Jessica snatched her arm back from the suddenly hostile guest. "I met Jackson at your party. I met Roland, too. I never pretended not to know them!"

"Wrong answer, my old friend." The words snarled from her lips as Emily planted her hands on the counter to rise. "Jackson never came down for dinner. I should know because I waited for him until midnight. I waited until I decided to come waste my time with you. His scent is on your skin and I know what that means. He's marked you as his own."

Jessica's heart plummeted into her shoes. There were a hundred ways she could look at her distraught friend's accusations, but they all led up to the same thing. Her Jackson was Emily's Jackson, and the thought of it tore her to pieces.

"Damn all this cloak and dagger crap." Jessica grabbed her goblet and splashed its contents into the sink with a rare outburst of frustration. She watched the wine run down the basin like the tears on her friend's cheek. She wondered why Jackson, and now Emily, brought out such primal emotions. "I would never intentionally hurt you, Em. I never have and I never will. Please believe me."

"I think I told you before. Maybe you listened and maybe you didn't. I don't know who to trust anymore. I'm leaving."

"Where are you going?" Jessica rushed around from the kitchen, attempting to press her palm on the door to prevent it from opening.

"You know what they say, right? About the Devil you know? At least I know the Hart clan."

"You know us, too." Jessica forced the words past her lips as Emily opened the blocked door easily. She realized a little too late the phrase didn't really work in her favor. Without one look over her shoulder the angry girl climbed into the town car that waited outside, idling silently.

She thought she might not be able to trust us and had the car wait, Jessica thought with a sinking heart. *And now her fears are confirmed.*

"Hey you guys, what's going on?" Lucy emerged again from the bedroom, this time shielding her own eyes from the light.

This really wasn't a conversation Jessica was looking forward to having.

Chapter 5

"She's turning too soon. We'll have to bring the medical equipment in." Meredith moved away from the observation glass to face Jackson. He barely heard her statement, his attention drawn to the containment room where Emily paced relentlessly across the foam padded floor of the sparse cell.

"Do you have any idea what could have happened if she stayed with those girls the other night? You're losing control of this situation and I don't think I have to remind you it could mean certain death for all of us."

"Yet you did just remind me, didn't you, Mother?" Jackson responded with a strong tone, his gaze dangerously intense. "I wanted Emily seated within the clan before she turned as much as you did. I know better than anyone we can't take chances right now, though I feel we must with her. Do you not think it's strange Emily hails from your very birthplace and yet we came across her on the other side of the country?"

He could almost feel the Dark Breed at his back, breathing down his neck and waiting for the opportunity to take him down the minute he lost control of his family. His hold was slipping away from him with every second Emily transitioned without a mate, and his bloodline lost faith in his ability to lead.

"We could test the formula on her," his mother whispered then, though even she sounded horrified by her own suggestion. "Roland brought this on himself when he found her in the mountains after the attack. He should have left her there to meet her fate with the others. Neither you nor I caused this."

"No!" Jackson slammed his fist against the glass with a force that sent a streamlined crack radiating out from the center of the impact.

The formula was a well-guarded secret known to only the most trusted of their inner circle. His father died developing it, and it was their only hope against the chaos of the Dark Breed clan who hunted them. Jackson had to protect that secret and keep his family line united and strong or they would all fall to the usurping feral pack.

"No, we don't know what it could do to her, what it can do to anyone like us." He instantly regained control of his emotions and watched the now-fractured image of the young girl who had hesitated when she heard the sound from the other side of the mirror. "Roland is family, something that you taught me well. He couldn't bear to leave the girl to the rogue who bit her, just as my father couldn't bring himself to murder Michael when he had the chance. We are all responsible for this."

"Never say his name in front of me!" Meredith hissed with a rare show of fury, but Jackson could see the pain in her eyes before she masked her emotions.

He watched as Emily pulled at her upswept hair in frustration and it fell over her shoulders in a thick mass of blond curls. Her evening dress was torn along the hem and her shoes were nowhere to be seen as she resumed her canter from one side of the room to the other. As loyal as he was to his family and their legacy, he was forced to admit that the image of Jessica's face haunted him.

"If it works, she'll stop changing," Meredith offered one last bit of advice before Jackson let her know in no uncertain terms that route was closed.

"If it doesn't, she'll die. Just like Father did."

•

"She still isn't answering and the wedding is supposed to be this weekend." Lucy frowned at her cell phone when the call to Emily went to voicemail again. "Do you want me to leave her another message?"

"I think if she hasn't responded to the first ten messages by now she doesn't intend to answer." Jessica tried to keep her attention on the winding road while at the same time looking at the scenery to see if they were even close to being on the right track.

She found it hard to believe the folks around town had no real idea about the location of the mansion, but the hills in that area were so secluded and remote she supposed a private location might stay pretty private with enough money to buy the security.

"Wait, I remember seeing that tree before we turned last time!" Lucy pointed, inadvertently blocking Jessica's view of the sharp bend in the road. It didn't help that Lucy had said the same thing five times already, or that Jessica automatically turned in the same direction to look.

The car drove off the pavement and the front left tire lodged in a soft, deep ditch filled with years of decomposing leaves and fertile soil.

Jessica seriously questioned her skills as a driver after two near misses that week. She looked over at her friend to make sure she was all right. Lucy had retracted her pointing finger quickly enough to cover her eyes with her hands and only peeked through them when everything grew still.

"Shew, that was a close one!" She popped the passenger side door open.

Jessica opened her own door only to discover a steep drop below her feet. After careful consideration, she decided to crawl through the same door as Lucy.

"I'm pretty sure we're in the right spot," the former backseat driver assured her in a cheery voice as she began to walk up the steep road.

"You mean right here, or all the other places we passed that you almost got us killed over?"

"Just keep walking and you'll see." Lucy smiled over her shoulder. Nothing ever seemed daunting to the girl.

They were in the middle of nowhere without a single bar of cell phone service, so Jessica decided to follow. They hadn't gone far before a shiver ran up her spine and she got the same feeling of eyes on her that she had experienced the night of the bridal dinner.

"I think you're right, Luce. This has to be the same area at least."

"Yeah, I know. The house is right up here like I said." The tone of her voice left no doubt, so Jessica was surprised when they encountered a gate with a no trespassing sign bolted on.

"The whole town is practically inside the forest," Lucy said and straddled the rail to climb over to the other side.

"Yes, I realize that, but we're looking for a castle, not a park ranger's station."

"You know I never get lost once I've been somewhere, right?"

Jessica felt like they were violating some kind of nature preserve, and the hair on the back of her neck stiffened again. "It looks like nobody has been out this way for months or more. The leaves and branches on the ground haven't even been disturbed. We were just here two days ago."

"I don't care. I know we're going the right direction." Lucy shrugged and resumed her hike.

That was enough for Jessica and she increased her pace to catch up. She didn't know where Lucy found the energy to get so far ahead because she was exhausted, having gotten very little rest the past few nights. She reminded herself that Lucy snored away most of that time on her very own bed while she laid awake.

They circled around the side of the mountain and the stone turrets of the manor house came into view once they cleared the trees. The black marble drive was just the way they remembered it, except it was now littered with dead leaves and tacky with pine cone sap as they walked across.

Though they had left the apartment that morning in search of the grounds, it was well into the afternoon by the time they found the place. The cold breeze and retreating sun reminded them it was already growing late.

"Let's just go in and get Emily," Jessica said with a little urgency. "I'll feel a lot better if we can talk to her in the daylight and give her the chance to come back with us if she wants."

She hadn't told Lucy about Jackson or Emily's feelings toward him. Part of her reason was to honestly shelter Lucy from the drama, but also she didn't want to admit her part in it all. If she had to be honest, she wasn't even sure what her part was.

Jessica resolved to try the front door first, just like it was a normal visit. She was caught off guard when she found the massive entryway standing open. Something seemed out of place though she couldn't put her finger on it as she watched the brittle leaves blow in from the yard onto the polished granite tiles of the foyer.

If this was truly Jackson's home, she didn't think he'd leave it open to the elements in such a way. The amount of damage any extended exposure to these conditions might cause to the paintings alone was terrible to consider.

"It's really dark in there," Jessica cautioned.

"That's why they make light switches!" Lucy fearlessly stepped into the thick shadows that engulfed the foyer just past the door.

"You can't just go bumbling into other people's houses like that when they aren't at home. I think there's a law against this!"

"Well, there's some kind of cord or chain thingy here." Lucy had made her way into the corner and pulled on the silken braid. The deep, resonating sound of a gong rang throughout the great hall, echoing off into the distance for what felt like an eternity.

"Now they'll know we're here if they didn't before." Jessica felt along the wall for a switch. When she found the round knob she pushed it in and a great shimmering light from the overhead chandelier bathed the room in a thousand sparkles. She immediately noticed all the furniture was draped with white sheets.

"Oh, look at that. They pack fast," Lucy breathed, turning around in a circle to see the entire layout.

Jessica followed her gaze, but she froze in alarm as her eyes focused on a tall figure lounging inside the door frame of what looked to be a library. She put a warning hand on Lucy's shoulder, but the careless girl paid her no heed and moved closer to the man.

His black eyes watched her wayward friend like an animal measuring up his prey as she approached. Jessica took a moment to regard his unusual attire, his black leather pants setting off a white, ruffled shirt open at the collar; it starkly contrasted against the hair on his chest above his casually folded arms. His black hair fell just past his shoulders and glistened in the chandelier light with a glossy luster. This man was beautiful, like all the other people she had met from the Hart family, but he had a wild look about him, rugged and uncivilized. She didn't think he belonged in the house any more than she and Lucy did.

She was at her friend's side almost immediately, but not before the dark stranger had taken Lucy's hand in one fluid motion and placed it to his full, sensual lips for a lingering kiss.

Lucy sighed and Jessica wished for once she'd use a little caution. Even if this character had no ill intentions, which she seriously doubted, Lucy would do well to play a little hard to get once in a while.

"A pleasure, my lady." His fingers lingered against the palm of Lucy's hand and Jessica thought the girl might collapse.

He then turned to Jessica who stiffly pushed herself between the stranger and her friend. He made a visible point to acknowledge her guarded stance and let her know he understood she wasn't willing to be the recipient of another advance.

"That's right," she assured him coldly when he gave her a knowing look. "I'm not your lady."

"Then whose lady might you be, may I inquire?" He moved gracefully away from the open doorway and walked silently around until he was behind her.

Every fiber in her being begged Jessica to spin about and not to keep this predator at her back, but she was stubborn and willed herself to remain in place, unwilling to give in to his intimidation.

"Let's see, shall we?" His soft, melodic voice was suddenly in her ear and she could feel his breath on the back of her neck.

She spun around with her fists in the air, but before she could land a punch Lucy was next to her, shoving the stranger off balance. "Get away from her, you creep!" she added for good measure, and the two girls stood side by side ready to fight.

"Jackson," he stated simply. His eyes locked with Jessica's as he crossed the room to a small marble table that rested against the wall. "He must have left this message for his driver to take to you. Right before he scurried away like a whelp with his tail between his legs."

Her stomach dropped when he spoke Jackson's name at first. This man knew a lot more about what was going on than she did and that made him dangerous.

"How do you know who I am?"

"I can read." His answer was short this time and he was clearly losing patience.

She palmed the heavy letter he tossed to her; her name was on the cover in Emily's writing. She began to urge Lucy toward the front door before they met the same questionable fate as Jackson's driver.

The moment they neared the exit, the leather-clad predator was in front of them with his arm barring the doorway. She expected the worst, but instead of a physical outburst the rogue gently captured Lucy's chin in the palm of his hand and gazed deeply into her eyes.

"You have strength after all, my beauty," he whispered so low it was barely audible to Jessica and she was standing right next to the girl. "I guarantee I will see you again."

It was her turn now to break her friend away from the mesmerizing voice of the stranger. He made no further attempt to stop them and Jessica didn't intend to give him any chances to change his mind as they hurried down the driveway.

A rustling sound in the woods seemed to keep pace with them as they backtracked on the forest trail, and Jessica was sure she heard a howl through the trees.

"There's a dog loose in the woods," Lucy mumbled. Jessica noticed with alarm that her lips were nearly blue from the cold and her skin was much paler than usual.

"It's okay. It's just a dog," Jessica assured, briskly rubbing her arms as they crossed the gate that blocked the trail from the road. She could see the car from there, the wheel mysteriously free from the ditch. Jessica had no explanation for the rescue and didn't want to wait around long enough to consider it. It was almost dark and a chorus of howls had added to the first lonely bay.

"Is it just a dog?" Lucy asked, then curled up in the front seat of the car and gently closed her eyes.

Chapter 6

"Read me the letter again, please?" Lucy begged her friend from her spot beneath the blanket on the small couch. Scruffy had been distraught ever since the girls arrived back from the manor house and spent all his time sniffing their clothes and attempting to lick Lucy's hands.

"It won't say anything different the second time around, I promise."

Jessica could barely believe the words on the page when she'd choked them out during the first reading. Emily told them she suffered from a rare illness that could often be debilitating at and she realized after the past weekend it was wrong to impose herself on her friends. She was certain the best place for her was with the Hart family doctors, where she would be cared for in a private setting. She finished the letter by bluntly stating that until they knew more about the nature of the affliction it would be best if she didn't have outside visitors.

"We're her family. We should get to see her, too," Lucy said from the couch. The sound of her voice was so desolate that Jessica looked up from the parchment to notice a light sheen of sweat on her friend's forehead.

"Are you still feeling sick?"

"Not as sick as Emily, apparently." The girl made a face but shivered under the covers.

Jessica put the note down and hurried across the room to lay the back of her hand on Lucy's cheek.

"Oh, quit that, I'm fine!"

"When did you get this?" Jessica leaned over the girl, capturing her wrist with a solid grip before turning her hand palm down. A large red welt stood out on her white skin, and the wound looked painful.

"I don't know," Lucy answered quietly, staring at the mark like she was seeing it for the first time. "Maybe I got into some nettles while we were walking back to the car? It was so cold I probably wouldn't have felt a thing."

"It could be, but then you'd probably have a rash. This kind of looks like a sting or a bite."

"Well, whatever it is, just give me some aspirin and a band-aid. It's late and we have to get moving." Lucy pushed the blankets off, wincing a little when the soft fabric came in contact with the back of her hand.

"I don't know where you think we're going, unless it's to the doctor's office. You're not well and the last thing we need is you flapping all around in the middle of a cold snap. Then I'll have two sick friends to worry about."

"Fine, then. We'll go by old Doc Sylar's place first thing in the morning. If I feel better then we can head to the airport right away."

"Are you out of your mind?" Jessica picked up the letter and waved it in Lucy's face. "She said she doesn't want us there when she's sick."

"Hey, I'm going to somebody's wedding! She went back to Seattle so I guess that's where she wanted to have it. This is Emily, remember? Do you really want to abandon her because she's sick, probably scared, and wrote us one little letter?"

"I know. Friends forever and always."

"You're really lucky you have me to remind you, Jess." Lucy started across the room only to have Scruffy press up against her legs every time she took a step.

"Speaking of little reminders ..." Jessica gestured toward Scruffy, sure he was smart enough to understand she was referring to him.

"Oh, yes!" Lucy bent down and rewarded the small dog with a hug and kiss. "My Granny's just going to love having you at her house for a while!"

•

A thousand thoughts vied for attention inside Jackson's mind as he traversed the halls of the remote hunting lodge near the Canadian wild lands, but his heart kept coming back to Jessica. Try as he might, he was unable to define the hold she had on him. If he could just find a way to understand his feelings for her, perhaps he would be able to control them. It wasn't as if he had a choice in the matter—his first responsibility was to his family.

He'd pulled everyone out of the manor house the moment Emily returned in the middle of the night and he'd seen the changes in her. Jackson had no idea how close their enemy was, but if she was turning without a mate and there was even one member of the Dark Breed within miles, they would know it. She was safer back in their territory—they all were. He'd hoped Emily and Roland would bond when they reached her hometown, something he had agreed to in an effort to facilitate the match. He believed it might have worked, too, if her transformation hadn't accelerated.

"Oh, you've got to be kidding me," he openly chided himself as his thoughts turned back to Jessica once again.

He shook his head to clear it as he came to Emily's observation chamber. The doctor was already inside, monitoring her vital signs and measuring her bone structure. To his surprise, there was another person in attendance as well.

Jackson leaned through the open doorway and motioned for Roland to join him on the other side of the glass. The man looked weary as he ran his fingers across his eyes.

"Tell me the truth, Roland. Tell me again what happened when you saw Emily in the mountains after the attack."

The blue-eyed male turned his back to the scene in the other room and rested lightly against the cold glass. Jackson towered over him by several inches, the dominant figure. Though Roland was at ease, his stance was still respectful.

"I could smell the blood a mile away that night. It was too close to our markers, and that was dangerous. I was careful when I approached, always staying downwind. I knew it could be a trap because Michael is well aware of our boundaries."

A displeased growl came from Jackson's throat in response to Roland's careless reference to the leader of the Dark Breed pack. The smaller man instinctively lowered his head in an act of submission before continuing.

"Then I saw her in the clearing, her clothing torn to shreds above her hiking boots. The moonlight washed over her perfect skin and even with the blood all over her body, even with the streaks of it threaded through her hair ... I thought she was so beautiful I couldn't breathe. I knew the Dark Breed had been there. I could catch their scent all over the forest floor but I didn't care."

"Tell me what you haven't told anyone else. I know you're holding something back," Jackson urged.

"She was dying, Jackson. Her heart had just stopped when I knelt by her in the moonlight and I breathed life into her with my own lips, knowing what she could become. I did it because I couldn't let her die!"

He stood up straight then with a look of defiance in his eyes that surprised the leader of the clan. He respected Roland's strength. And Jackson was beginning to know exactly what it was like to feel that strongly for a woman.

"I thought you didn't want this match," he said with a curious look in his eyes. "Why did you scout Emily's friend at the party?"

"Emily deserves better than me. She rejected the match the moment you made it. I thought if I could move on somehow, even just try, she could have the chance to be happy with another man. That's all I could want for her, but the effort was ridiculous. I followed that friend of hers to Emily's room, just to see what she would tell me when she emerged. Of course, I already knew what she would say. Emily doesn't love me."

"Does she know you're the one who saved her?" he asked. It was against their laws to revive a victim who succumbed from wounds inflicted by their kind. He would not have spoken about it to anyone, let alone the innocent soul he was trying to save.

"The only thing she even remembers is hiking the trail. When she woke you were standing next to her bed with the doctor. You were the first person she saw, an unmated male and leader of the clan at that. Of course she tried to bond to you, probably without understanding what she was feeling."

Jackson knew he should be furious with Roland for the reference to the fact that not only was he not mated, but he was head of the family and neglecting his duty in that respect. He tried to temper his reaction with the obvious truth. If he had bonded by now, as was proper for the leader of a clan, Emily wouldn't have fixated on him so easily.

"Come with me." Jackson led the way, motioning over his shoulder for Roland to follow him into Emily's room.

The doctor moved back and stood at a respectful distance as Jackson approached her bedside. She looked up at him and smiled radiantly, but he responded with a neutral, curt nod.

"You have a visitor," Jackson said, feeling a little uncomfortable as she reached for him with her right hand.

"Yes, I can see that." Emily looked into his eyes.

"Actually, Roland is here to see you. I need him to help me sort through some family business, so please don't keep him long. His work is very important, but he asked if he could spend a few moments with you first. I was forced to agree, as he was the one who saved your life to begin with."

He kept his voice as sincere as possible, and though he wanted Emily to understand how important her visitor was in the family, he did actually need Roland. He needed him to take ownership of his woman so they could settle this matter permanently. A look of confusion crossed her face as he stepped aside, but Roland came forward to take her hand that still lingered off the edge of the bed. "You asked to spend time with me? I didn't know it was you who brought me down from the mountain. I never thanked you, I guess." She wrapped her fingers around the young man's hand.

Jackson backed out of the room with such silent grace that none of the occupants noticed save the doctor, who nodded at the clan leader with a knowing smile. He was almost overwhelmed by a strong feeling of satisfaction. It had been so long since he had made any positive gain as the new head of the family.

He missed his father terribly at that moment, wondering what he could have done differently to prevent the recent chaos that had arisen since his death. Michael hadn't dared to cross the line when he was still alive. Jackson could only assume that it was out of some lingering respect for the patriarch of the clan. The renegade leader hadn't shown him the same consideration, though Jackson couldn't have killed his own brother any more easily than their father could have.

Jackson wished he could tell Michael how their father died for him. How he developed a dangerously unstable formula that could stop a shifter from changing, if only he could test it. He refused to try it on any of them, feeling personally responsible for the formula's need to begin with, so he administered it to himself. His father would never change again. He was dead. And all for the love of a disobedient son who split from the clan and defied them all with his careless recruiting and carnal passions.

It was uncivilized. The only consolation he was able to find at the moment was the fact that he had left Jessica far behind and well away from the danger his family faced. He really didn't know what he'd do if Michael found out about his feelings for her, or how far he'd go to protect her.

Chapter 7

"My arm still hurts," Lucy complained as she pulled her suitcase along the sidewalk to the car rental agency on the far side of the airport. She winced every time the wheels went over a crack and Jessica noticed she was having trouble keeping up. It was usually the other way around.

"Well, you did get a rabies shot yesterday. The doc told you not to travel for at least a week, not that you'd take anybody's advice."

"I waited a whole day, didn't I? Besides, he was obviously crazy I think. I mean, nothing bit me. Did you see anything bite me?" Lucy didn't even put up a fight when Jessica grabbed the handle from her and easily piloted both overnight bags toward the glass door of the car pick up.

"No, I didn't see anything bite you," Jessica said as she held the door. "But like he said, you're better safe than sorry, right? When is the last time you had a rabies shot, anyway? I mean, I've seen the guys you've dated in the past ..."

"Oh ha ha. Very funny. At least I can get a date."

"That's true. I seem to remember I was your last date, Miss Smarty-pants. Besides, when I choose a guy this time I want to make sure he's special. I don't want there to be any room left in my heart for doubt or unhappiness when I share it again."

"Dude, that's beautiful," Lucy said wryly. "Remind me to write Hallmark when we get home."

"We have to get where we're going before we can go back," Jessica reminded her friend, who was now doing her best to recline in the hard plastic waiting room chairs while she filled out the paperwork.

"Do you need me to show you how to get the truck into four

wheel drive?" The eager young attendant held out a set of keys, his eyes all over Lucy who was clearly not dressed for a wilderness outing in her long velvet skirt and high-heeled boots.

"We're from Ohio. We can drive in the snow," Jessica answered as she dislodged the heavy key ring from his grip.

"You think it snows in Ohio? You do realize you're headed into northern Washington. If you even make it up there, you'll never get out."

"What's that supposed to mean?"

"There's a storm coming in, that's all. You ladies get to where you're going right away and stay there. It isn't safe to be trying to go up those mountain roads in any condition, let alone with a foot of snow on 'em. Heck, they probably won't be open for long anyway. If you find yourself without a place to stay, you can always come back here. I have a big bed in my apartment."

"You sure your momma will let you have a girl overnight?" Lucy stood to let Jessica know she was ready to get going.

He grinned back at her. "But seriously, there's a box in the back of the truck with a flashlight, road flares, bottled water and a few candles. Hopefully you won't need it, but you can't be too careful."

•

The hair on the back of Jackson's neck stiffened as he came across unfamiliar tracks near the edge of the wilderness that marked the Hart Clan boundaries. These were clearly foreign and any encroachment by outsiders put his family at risk.

He couldn't look the other way any longer. Michael's ravenous appetite for new blood was obviously increasing, though the very thing that made his brother so different was something Jackson struggled with everyday. How was the leader of the Dark Blood pack able to be with so many women without bonding? Jackson knew if he were to choose a mate himself, she would be part of him for the rest of his life. Yet Michael proliferated with no sign or remorse or attachment to any one person, and his followers grew rapidly.

His heart ached for the child he loved so much as they were growing up. It was true Michael had always been troubled, a dark and brooding boy. But Jackson saw the beautiful side of his soul as well. His amazing artistic productions were the result of his deep and often over-the-top passions. He thought for a time his little brother was a genius, but it became clear as he grew older that his brilliant sculptures, murals and musical projects came fewer and farther between his manic episodes.

The prints in the snow continued as far as Jackson was able to pick them up with his limited senses. His stomach clenched when he remembered the ranger station that sat at the edge of the conservation area and protected the wildlife in their private preserve. The Hart Clan donated a fortune to national preserves all over the country, though their reasons were as private; they needed the land to survive on.

Would Michael dare to take the lives of the innocent rangers who kept acres of untamed wilderness safe for all of their kind?

The thought twisted his gut into a thousand knots, for in truth, he didn't know how far Michael would go anymore. He needed to reach the outpost as quickly as possible to ascertain its condition. There was only one way to cover that much ground in a limited amount of time. Jackson's skin began to tingle even before he consciously made the decision to shift. He wanted to run free, to let the primal side of his existence take over. His soul needed to live in a state without a care about the right or wrong feelings he had for Jessica. All his desires were justified as he dropped to his hands and knees on the forest floor.

The heart of the wolf who loved her made no excuses. None were necessary.

•

"There's a cell tower. Pull over quick!"

"Do you really think I'm falling for that one again?" Jessica asked after far too many hours in the car with Lucy. Add the snow that had been falling in the past hour or so and the poor visibility, and she was gripping the steering wheel with white knuckles.

"It really is this time. Look." Lucy held out her mobile phone and Jessica could see the message light flashing on the tiny display. "Just pull over for a second so I don't lose the connection while I check."

"Sure, what's another ten minutes in the middle of an eternal journey of white despair? I can't really tell where to pull over."

Lucy bit down on the fingertips of her right glove and pulled it off her hand, wincing when it slid over her wound. Jessica thought it should be getting better, but it didn't appear to have lessened since their visit to the doctor. Lucy seemed to be in better spirits, though.

"Jason called again. Look at this, Jess! Ten messages and five of them are his. That's crazy. Oh, here's one from Granny." Lucy pulled the display back and dialed her voicemail.

Jessica watched her friend's face crumple as she listened to the remote message on the phone. She knew it was serious when the girl quietly hit the save button and flipped the display closed. The mood had changed drastically and Jessica was afraid to ask what was wrong.

"Granny said Scruffy ran away almost an hour after we dropped him off. She feels terrible and is calling the pound every hour in case someone brings him in. She hung up fliers all over the neighborhood, but thinks it's so cold out that he's probably holed up somewhere keeping warm."

"Oh God." Jessica put her face in her hands and rested her forehead on the steering wheel so Lucy wouldn't see her tears. "The one thing I choose to be responsible for when I move back home, and I lose him because I decide to take a road trip. I should have brought him with us."

"There's no way they would have let him on the plane. He had no papers, no shot records and hadn't even been fixed. I didn't want to say anything at first, but he probably has fleas, too! This isn't your fault. When we get back he'll be sitting right outside your door waiting for you."

"That's all I need, a pupsicle on my doorstep to remind me of my failures when I get home."

"He survived long before you picked him up and brought him to your apartment."

"Yes, he did," Jessica conceded, her thoughts instantly turning to the day she met Jackson for the first time and how the encounter had made her feel. A lot of strange things happened after that, but she couldn't change the way he affected her.

"Why don't you use your dating service phone there to call someone and find out where we are? This stupid rental doesn't have Onstar and we should have been somewhere near our hotel at least an hour ago."

"If we don't have GPS ourselves, how is anyone supposed to find us? Just keep going and we'll get there. It's a good thing you filled up at that last gas station when we got off the highway." Lucy nodded in what was supposed to be a reassuring manner, but stopped when she noticed the horrified look on Jessica's face.

"When did we get off the highway exactly?" Her grip on the wheel increased.

"After you got gas, silly." Lucy nodded as she spoke. "You took the fork that branched off to the right instead of the left."

"And you noticed that at the time? I thought you never got lost?"

"I never get lost if I've been someplace before! I've never even been to the state of Washington, you know. We're still going north anyway. Hey, we could even be in Canada by now."

Jessica looked again at the rearview mirror that also displayed the temperature and direction. The compass was one of the reasons she hadn't known they were driving on the wrong road for so long.

"So, in theory, we just have to find a road that goes west and we'll probably connect with the highway again in no time."

"Sounds good to me," Lucy said without a hint of worry in her voice. "We can stop at that house up ahead and ask for directions. I can see a light on, so somebody's probably home."

Jessica squinted through the white haze and saw a thick tree line ahead. There was some kind of light in the distance and it was a warm, welcoming glow that had her sighing in relief. Ice had formed on the wiper blades as they sat there, so after a few passes they had to get out and run the ice scraper over the rubber before they could see out of the windshield again. She didn't want to alarm Lucy, but it was getting dark a lot quicker than she'd anticipated.

They got the truck in motion and moved slowly toward the light that flickered behind the deep green pines. They hadn't gone far before Jessica was able to make out the no trespassing sign posted to a gate that designated the area as a private nature reserve.

"Now what do we do, turn around?" Jessica tried to keep the panic out of her voice. It had been a long time since they gassed up at the last station and she couldn't recall seeing any buildings along the road after that.

"Drive the truck around the gate," Lucy said like the answer should have been obvious. "We have four wheel drive and it isn't far off the path."

"And just forget the no trespassing sign?"

"That's only for hunters. We need directions. Look at it this way—if someone stops us for trespassing, we can at least ask them where we are and how to get back."

No matter which way she viewed it, Jessica couldn't refute Lucy's logic. She pressed the four wheel up button and slowly navigated them around the gate, praying there were no holes or ditches camouflaged by so much snow.

Jessica couldn't tell the road from the rest of the plain in all the snow very well, so she inched ahead slowly toward the opening in the trees where the soft glow lighted their way like a beacon.

"If anyone lives out here, they haven't left since at least the last blizzard," Jessica said. "There are no tire tracks here at all."

"Maybe it's their job to stay there all winter?"

"What kind of job is that—a ski instructor or igloo builder? Maybe a dog sled trainer?"

"Park Ranger, obviously," Lucy said, though as soon as she answered Jessica could see the sign for herself. It clearly read *Ranger Station 749.*

Chapter 8

"Crap. I knew this was going to happen!"

Jessica shifted the truck into reverse. She gained a few inches of ground before the snow-covered ditch captured the front driver's side tire again. A little play forward and back did nothing to free them of their situation and only managed to dig them in deeper.

"Is it in four-wheel drive?" Lucy leaned forward to peer at the knobs and dials on the dash, but had to brace herself when Jessica gunned it one last time.

"Oh gosh, I don't know! I'm only a girl from Ohio. Maybe we should call your friend back at the car rental agency?"

"Of course it is. I'm sorry," Lucy looked at her sheepishly. "He'd probably like it if we called him, though. Do you think he'd come and get us?"

"I'd rather trek through the arctic tundra in my pajamas than spend one night in his bed with his mother in the next room."

"You're probably right. I'll bet he's busy tonight anyway. You know how much internet gaming goes on with EverQuest over the weekends. So many dungeons and dragons, so little time." Lucy ran her gloved hand over the interior of the foggy windshield. "I don't think it's far up the road to the station. We'll just walk the rest of the way."

"Provided the light we saw through the trees is it. We don't really know for sure where the building is actually located."

"There's only one way to find out." Lucy pulled out her phone charger and plugged it into the lighter socket on the truck. "We're not getting anywhere here as it is, just more hot air steaming up the glass. My cell just died anyway, so I'll charge it while we go look."

Jessica was forced to admit that her friend had a valid point.

They were stuck in the ditch with little else to do, but she intended to keep the truck running and the headlights on so they wouldn't lose their way if the ranger station wasn't just inside the forest. She knew it wasn't smart to wander very far in the middle of a snowstorm, but she also thought there wasn't much chance the private reserve saw a lot of traffic during the winter months so help wasn't likely to come along.

She carefully climbed out of the driver's side door, planting one foot on the rail of the truck and easing the other down into the ditch. She was alarmed when her fur-trimmed boot broke through the crusted top of the drift and she found herself knee-deep in the cold powder.

Lucy stood near the right headlight, her velvet scarf completely covering her head and shoulders. The snow was shallower on the level road. She took a moment to marvel at the pure beauty of the winter wonderland surrounding them—until a sharp gust of bitterly cold wind whipped across the open field and howled through the trees ahead like a banshee.

Jessica grabbed Lucy's hand as they made their way toward the distant glow. Before they'd traveled a few dozen steps she turned around to gauge their progress. The headlights were already dim in the distance and she wondered if it was an effect from the snow or the truck battery giving out.

I hope it's still idling, she thought to herself. The wind quickened and even though she strained to hear the engine she'd left running, she couldn't be sure if it was with the storm whipping through the trees.

"Did you hear that?" Lucy pulled on her hand and she came close to hear what she was trying to say. "I think I heard a dog howling just ahead."

"It's just the wind, I'm sure," she reassured, but even as she said the words they felt uncertain on her lips.

The forest of pines grew closer as they struggled ahead, but the light stayed on within their boughs and gave her a little hope. They stayed on course. If they concentrated on the sides of the road she could see they were lined by a slight dip that must be the ditch she'd driven into.

There was another gate and sign set up right against the trees, but it was hard for Jessica to read the warnings. It was nearly dark.

If the ranger station wasn't nearby, they were definitely in trouble. She turned to look the way they'd come, but even the footprints from their recent passage were all but erased.

They passed through the gate unchecked and under the massive boughs of the ancient pine trees the forest interior enjoyed a bit of relief from the elements. The girls could follow the trail now, even though it was much darker inside the protective foliage.

Jessica thought she could make out the outline of a building ahead and it spurred her into action. She wrapped her arm around Lucy's waist and pulled her along. It was still freezing cold, but the break from the harsh wind made all the difference and they moved quickly along the path.

Twigs snapped and cracked all around them, and a few times she thought she saw the flash of nocturnal eyes deep in the brush that tangled its way through the trees.

This is a wildlife preserve, after all! She carefully kept her thoughts to herself in an effort save Lucy from unnecessary distress.

It was almost dark when they reached the clearing, and a four wheel drive truck sat quietly under a blanket of snow near the front porch. They stepped onto the porch, slipping on the wooden surface slick with a dusting of snow. Though no outside light was on, the two women could clearly see a number of animal tracks disturbing the white powder on the brittle lumber planks. They gingerly stepped across the creaking boards and Jessica knocked on the roughly hewn wooden door. It was sturdy, even heavy, but the pressure from her knuckles pushed the door open a few more inches.

"Hello?" she called through the small access, and even that tiny crack bathed her frigid skin with light and warmth.

"Come on, let's go in." Lucy pushed past her, eager to share some of the shelter that lay just beyond the door.

"Lucy!" Jessica said from the threshold, but she was hard-pressed to refuse the comfort the cabin offered as her friend swept inside. "What if someone lives here?"

"If someone does live here they're rangers. It's their job to take care of us, you know."

Jessica hesitated a moment, then decided if someone did actually reside there it was rude to leave the door open and let out all the wonderful heat. She stepped inside and pulled it closed. She heard the bolt automatically click into place when something heavy crashed onto the porch where she had just been standing.

She stifled a gasp and turned to Lucy who looked just as alarmed.

"Maybe a tree limb came down came down from all the snow?"

"It must have been aiming for me, then," Jessica said.

After a quick look out the window revealed nothing on the porch, she reached for the deadbolt to make sure it was securely locked. A small amount of snow drifted past the threshold when it was exposed earlier, and it soaked the rug on the hardwood floor at her feet.

"Maybe we shouldn't throw the bolt." Jess put her fingers on the cold brass, about to turn it back when Lucy made a sour face.

"What is that smell? Something's burning." She covered her nose and mouth with a black velvet glove and walked over to the fireplace. Jessica joined her, but there was nothing in the hearth except a few orange coals left from a fire that had burned hot not too long ago.

"Nothing unusual here. Where's the kitchen?" She picked up on the scent Lucy was noticing closer to the next room and they entered a small area with a tiny cooking station, a table and two chairs.

"What the heck?" Jessica almost gagged as they approached the smoking pan on one of the double burners. She wrapped her scarf around her hand and grabbed the pot by the handle, moving it away while Lucy turned off the heat.

"Dinner's ready," she exclaimed brightly as they both peered inside at the charred remains of what might have been beef stew at one time. There was almost nothing left to burn, so the Teflon itself was giving off the oily stench.

"Why would they leave the stove on?" Lucy said. "Look, there's even half a beer here. Oh, do you think they have more beer?"

Before Jessica could lecture her friend again on breaking and entering, Lucy had crossed the room and opened the door of the refrigerator to reveal a well-stocked spread that would last though quite a few winter storms.

"Too much food stuffed inside to fit beer. I'll bet they keep it in a cellar or on the back porch. You know, like Granny does," Lucy said. Jessica thought she might be losing her mind as the girl moved to the back door and popped the lock on the knob.

"I don't think it's a good idea to go outside now that's its dark." She desperately wanted to stop her from opening the back door. "We don't know what kind of animal might be lurking out there."

"Oh, I know what you mean. There could be lions and tigers and bears, oh my."

"I'm serious, Lucy. We don't know what happened to the rangers and I have a really bad feeling. Something about this place just doesn't seem right."

"Okay, there is something weird going on." Jessica sighed with relief when Lucy took her hand from the door and turned to face her. "But I think sometimes you worry too much. It's just a beer run. What could possibly happen?"

Lucy flipped her hair over her shoulder and reached for the knob. Before Jessica could stop her, she pulled the door inward with her left hand and pressed the switch for the outdoor light at the same time.

She actually took a step forward before she saw the hunched, shadowy figure of a wild animal at the edge of the porch.

"Jess!" she whispered with terror in her voice, finally subdued.

The beast crouched low in the darkness, a beautiful brown and grey wolf with taut muscles ready to spring onto its prey. Jessica was mesmerized by the pure strength and power the mere presence of the animal commanded, but she forced her legs to move.

The awesome creature growled low, a warning perhaps, but Jessica couldn't leave her friend alone in the doorway. She knew without a doubt she had never been in a more dangerous situation in her life, but she had always been her friend's protector. Nothing would ever change that.

Jessica slowly and gently put her hand over Lucy's fingers and slid her grip off the silver door knob. For one fleeting moment the massive wolf released Lucy's gaze and looked directly in Jessica's eyes. With that single look she knew without doubt she shouldn't be afraid. This wolf would never hurt her. In fact, he would protect her with all of his power. She reached for the handle that Lucy had released and began to open the door wider.

"Jess! What are you doing?" Lucy screamed, rudely jerking

her out of her calm and trusting state of being. The startled girl slammed the door shut and locked it instantly.

The wolf howled in despair as the barrier closed.

Jessica had never heard a more sorrowful sound.

◆

Sharp, stinging pain jabbed at the soles of his feet as Jackson lay hunched over on the ground near the woodshed at the ranger station. His body struggled with his mind in a war he knew he could not win. His feral senses told him that a member of the Dark Breed pack was inside the cabin and he could clearly catch the scent of human death through the trees in the distance.

He had been prepared for a fight to the finish and indeed, he welcomed it!

The outlaws trespassed upon his land, his private sanctuary, and murdered the innocents they employed to protect the preserve. Every fiber in his being strained to show the interlopers that he was the dominant head of his clan. He had never felt more perfectly alive than he did at that moment, when his heart pumped blood through his veins so hard all he could hear were the glorious drums of battle.

Ah, and then he saw past the furious bloodlust to her face. He was so startled by her presence that he nearly shifted out of form right then and there.

Damn, was he was no better than an adolescent learning to change for the first time? How had he missed her unique scent as he tracked the renegade pack to the very cabin where she was?

His heart swelled at the sight of her in the door and at that moment all desire for the fight was gone. He looked her directly in the eye and knew then she wasn't afraid of him. How could she be? The only thing she could have seen through his animal eyes was the pure and basic emotion of his love for her.

He'd barely made it to the outbuilding before he changed on the ramp that led up to the small barn.

Jackson was stunned by the speed in which he shifted. It had taken him by surprise, but the pure feeling of elation he felt at the moment he saw Jessica's face stayed with him.

He was a strong man, the strongest man of their clan, and yet he lay in the snow like a newborn, his heart beating with a desire that had nothing to do with the trouble that could be around the corner.

Dammit all, what was he thinking? Jessica was in terrible danger and he was willing to bet everything that she had no idea.

He pulled himself upright and entered the code in the combination lock on the shed door. He had emergency clothing inside, and though he'd never used this location to change before, he knew what supplies the rangers were required to keep.

Once he was fully outfitted, Jackson crossed the back lawn of the property with swift strides. He was properly dressed, but he still felt vulnerable as he always did when he shifted back and was forced to adjust to a narrower range of senses.

He paused on the first step of the front porch to draw a deep breath.

This is ridiculous! He was standing at the door step like a nervous teenager on prom night. This was essentially his house and by arriving in his domain Jessica put herself under his guard whether she meant to or not. With resolve, he took two long steps across the creaking wooden planks and knocked firmly on the door.

Chapter 9

"Jess, I don't feel so good." Lucy clutched her stomach and swayed slightly on her feet before she came to rest against the refrigerator next to the locked door.

She could understand where her friend was coming from. Jessica felt a little light-headed herself, once the shock of seeing a wild animal on the porch had faded. Lucy looked the worse for wear, however. At first she had truly appeared to feel better after their trip to the doctor. Now she was showing signs of the same illness she had before they left.

"I never should have agreed to this wild goose chase to start with." The words slipped unbidden through Jessica's lips as she watched Lucy pull her coat off and begin to scratch the skin on her arms through her blouse. Her friend was normally pale, but her skin appeared waxy now and a light sheen of sweat beaded up on her forehead.

"No, we had to come. We're the only family Emily has left and I refuse to forget about her when things get a little weird or tough. And I want you to know I wouldn't leave you behind either." She hung her coat on the back of the nearest kitchen chair.

And if I were a better friend I wouldn't have allowed you to wander off into the frozen tundra when the doc told me you shouldn't travel, Jessica thought, *and all for a remote chance to see Jackson again. I must be crazy! I doubt he'd even remember me.*

"We're here now, anyway." Lucy attempted a brave smile. "I'll grab a bottle of water and some Advil. Let me take a quick nap, you fix the fire up and we'll be good to go in no time, really. Maybe the rangers will even be back by then."

"That sounds like a plan," she struggled to remain calm as the realization of their circumstance hit home. Good Lord, they were in the middle of nowhere and her friend was sick. Still, someone had to be levelheaded and she'd be a monkey's uncle if that person turned out to be Lucy.

"I can think of worse things a forest ranger might find after a night out than a cute redhead tucked snugly into his bead," Jessica said to lighten the mood.

"Better than finding his kitchen half burned down, right? See, we're already doing them a favor by being here," Lucy agreed as she began opening doors in search of a bedroom.

After discovering a broom closet, they found a cozy place for Lucy to lie down. She curled up on top of the bedspread so Jessica pulled a quilt off the back of a nearby rocker and covered the shivering girl. The room was small with just a single window next to the bed. The glass was so heavily frosted with crystals she could barely see through the pane.

Lucy pleaded with her to shut the door, claiming the light from the fire Jessica stoked might keep her awake. The tiny space was so warm she agreed and gently closed the door until she heard the latch click into place.

Though the fire was a huge priority, Jessica had another as she retraced her steps to the kitchen. There had been an older looking phone on the wall and the first thing she wanted to do was see if it worked. She picked up the plastic receiver and put it to her ear. Static coursed through the connection and even though she was disappointed it wasn't functional, she knew the storm might have just caused a temporary outage. Feeling a little like a criminal, she slid open the drawers around the kitchen and utility area in search of a cell phone. Lucy had left hers in the car.

With little left to do, Jessica moved to the living room and knelt by the stone fireplace. In any other situation this would have been an unbelievably romantic spot. The coal bed still glowed with a deep orange light, and as she fed kindling to the remains of the fire, it leapt to life.

Feeling satisfied with some type of accomplishment, she rocked back on her heels at the same moment heavy footsteps pounded with determination across the frozen boards of the porch out front. There was no mistaking the stride of a man in a heavy boot. She jumped to her feet.

Thank God the park rangers are back! she thought with relief as she crossed the hardwood floor to throw the bolt on the heavy brass lock.

•

Jackson heard the lock click back at the same moment the back of his hand grazed the wood. Though he wanted to rush inside and capture Jessica in his arms he was paralyzed when the door flew open unexpectedly. Everything he'd imagined wasn't happening the way he'd thought, and for a man who was always in control he found he was at a rare loss.

The first things he saw were her beautiful eyes, at first filled with confusion, but then growing wide when she recognized his face in the darkened doorway. Her perfect mouth formed an O and his heart was torn apart when she covered her expression with a sheepskin glove. All his fantasies of a kiss between them were quelled.

"May I come in?" Jackson allowed the first pleasantry that entered his mind to escape his lips.

Did you just say that? Did you just ask to come in to your own house? He was clearly struggling with new emotions. His dominance over any situation was never a question before now. Jackson's duty was always clear-cut and this woman blurred lines he never knew existed before a few days ago.

"What are you doing here?" Her expression was so incredulous that even he questioned what brought him to the cabin on a night like tonight. It served to remind him that danger lurked nearby. At the very heart of his being he wanted to protect her more than anything else in the world.

"This is my property. Do you think we could talk about it inside?" He edged the door open a few more inches. She'd been smart enough to get a fire going in the brazier.

"You're a forest ranger?" She probably didn't intend to keep him from entering, but her surprising response almost made him laugh out loud. If only she knew who he was ...

And if I can be strong enough she never will, he pledged earnestly to himself. The surest way to keep her safe is to alienate her.

"I never thought I'd see you again," she said with such a raw and honest tone that it raked across his heart. His resolve wavered.

Jackson stepped inside and reached behind his back to close the door. What happened now was important and he must maintain control at all cost. This innocent woman, this beauty just inches away from his fingertips, depended on him to survive even if she didn't know it.

Though he was in his human form, he could still catch the scent of the renegade pack in the air. Multiple transgressors circled this cabin on a wide perimeter, but it wouldn't be long before they closed in on their prey.

Prey they would never have the luxury of tasting.

These rogues wouldn't dare cross him in person. Their crimes were always committed far from his reach, though Jackson had to admit they grew bolder every day. The fact they were so close now gave him pause and forced him to recalculate his strategy. He knew without hesitation that he would die to protect Jessica. He just hoped Michael and his pack didn't know that.

"Lucy's in the other room and she's not feeling well at all." Jessica reached out and set a gloved hand on his forearm. "I think she's going to need a doctor." Even through layers of wool and fabric, her touch inflamed him. He didn't want to fail her.

"I'm actually not a ranger, but my family does provide the preserve you see all around us, and we do have a doctor on staff," he finally answered. "I'm curious as to how you got here as well, I must admit, though I'm not displeased."

She blushed when he said that and he wondered how anyone could be so perfectly transparent with their emotions. Where he came from, strength was the all-important quality. Dominance was the key to survival. Though upon consideration, he was forced to admit there was always a legendary woman behind each patriarchal head of the family.

Jackson thought of his own mother, Meredith, and her considerable influence with the clan long after his father had passed on. For a fleeting moment his heart wrenched for the woman who gave birth to him, for the agony any one of the pack must feel when they outlived a mate. His stance must have softened or his eyes might have given away the sentimental thought, because Jessica smiled and gave his arm a reassuring squeeze.

And oh, how her smile was like a thousand lights in the twilight sky! If he never saw another thing in his life this would be enough to last him until the end. This was the very thing he came to protect, and despite his pledge to remain distant he covered her gloved hand with his own naked fingers.

He never should have touched her.

Jessica leaned in a little when he accepted her gesture, her face upturned. His fingers wrapped around her glove and pulled with determination to free her skin. He knew then all the control belonged to the dark-haired woman standing in front of him.

Everything he ever wanted, everything he never dared to dream could be his. She was standing in front of him. At that moment, no one other thing in the universe mattered. Though he hadn't moved at all he found she was pressed against his body, their hands entwined, crushed against their heartbeats that matched in passion.

This need went against everything Jackson believed in. He was aware he couldn't slake this raging lust that slammed through his body. She was not his match, could not be, and so he must forfeit the hunt. He knew the sanctity of the wisdom behind the ancient law that governed his kind, but his heart refused to let go. His left arm slid around her waist and held her close with a desire that could not be stopped by any rule.

Jackson raised his right hand and ran the back of his fingers along Jessica's cheek, fanning into the silken hair above her ear until they reached the back of her head. He clenched his fist firmly against the base of her skull, pulling enough to make her gasp with pleasure.

The moment her lips parted Jackson smothered them possessively with his mouth. He had to be careful with the delicate woman in front of him, but he couldn't stop himself from taking everything he needed from her kiss. She ardently gave him all she was made of, as he pulled what she had to offer to the surface for a taste.

A sharp sound in the distance struck brutally through the haze of Jackson's bliss and the protector in him snapped on guard. He broke away from Jessica long enough to hear the sound of breaking glass as it shattered to the floor inside one of the adjacent rooms.

She was dazed, but the woman was damn smart and she knew there was danger when he pushed her away. God, he couldn't help but marvel at this female who wasn't slighted by his response.

Jackson silently crossed the room, motioning for Jessica to remain where they had just embraced. One quick look into the kitchen let him know it hadn't been the point of breach.

That left only one place ...

"Lucy!" Jessica exclaimed with sudden realization, rushing forward before Jackson could react. She threw open the door to the small bedroom, but turned to him when the truth was revealed.

The bed was empty, the country quilt flung to the floor and the bedding disturbed. Pieces of sharp glass lined the window sill like vicious frozen teeth. Firelight from the living room made the blood on the jagged edges dance like it was alive and Jessica sunk to her knees.

Jackson moved forward, swiping his finger against one of the crimson rivulets before bringing it to his nose. This wasn't Lucy's blood—he was sure of it.

He did know who it belonged to, however. He knew who had taken Lucy from her bed in the dead of night and shivered at the thought of what Michael might do to her.

Chapter 10

"She doesn't have her coat." Jessica twisted the heavy velvet fabric between her fingers as she wrung her hands with worry. "She'll freeze if we don't find her."

Jackson knew time was crucial if he was to find Jessica's young friend alive at the end of his hunt. He grabbed a flashlight from the closet while he thought about his options. He could see well enough in the moonlight, but Jessica didn't know that.

"Jackson, there's a wolf outside—a big one. We have to be careful!"

Oh yes, I know very well there's a wolf out there, he thought to himself.

"I need you stay inside while I go around the back to see if she's gotten far." Jackson's tone was stern, commanding. She was already putting on her coat. The truth was he couldn't risk her seeing something she wouldn't understand, or worse, finding Lucy in pieces, scattered over the back lawn.

"You need someone to watch your back, let me come with you and at least try to help, please." Her voice wavered and he knew it would be a terrible thing for her to sit and do nothing while the fate of her friend hung in the balance.

"You'll only slow me down," Jackson said. His words were straightforward and she visibly flinched when he looked her in the eye.

Though it broke his heart to see the damage his command did, it was the truth. She would track up the snow, mix her scent with Lucy's on the trail. And if it came right down to it and he was forced to fight, she was a liability he couldn't afford. There was no doubt in his mind he'd choose Jessica's life over that of her friend's if there was no other way.

"You have to stay here in case the rangers come back so you can tell them what happened." Jackson smoothly misdirected her, and felt black-hearted for lying even if it was for her own safety. He knew perfectly well the rescue party was probably already dead. "In any case, I don't intend to be long. I want to see if she's nearby before we get more help."

"The glass was broken from the outside, Jackson. It was on the floor next to the nightstand and I saw blood on the shards. We need to call the police!"

She obviously didn't have a cell phone with her or she would have done that by now. It was a risky prospect, letting a family call go to 911, and he didn't want to chance that Jessica's report might be directed to someone other than the sensible local sheriff who let the Hart clan handle their own business.

"Lock the door once I'm outside and don't open it up for anyone but me," he instructed, forced to duck through the smaller frame that led onto the back porch.

"But, what if the rangers come back?" she said as he stepped out into the snow, purposefully obliterating his own wolf tracks from earlier.

She is so damn smart, Jackson thought to himself. He was going to have to be more careful with the things he said or she'd catch on to the truth.

"The rangers will have a key. They live here, remember? Now close the door."

•

Jackson moved silently over the crisp snow. Now that the storm lulled, the moonlight sparkled on the white crystals that coated the ground in the clearing around the cabin. He could see several different tracks at the edge of the yard, but only one set left a trail all the way to the windowsill. For a moment he wasn't sure what he was seeing, but after further inspection he understood what had transpired outside Lucy's bedroom.

Michael's scent lingered in the area and there were signs he had shifted right in front of the window as the girl slept. Large, bare footprints melted the snow all the way down to the frozen grass on the ground and Jackson wondered how long his brother had stood outside looking in.

Jackson saw where he'd broken the glass to unlock the pane. That was when he cut himself, but then he carefully lifted the damaged sill so that Lucy wouldn't suffer injury before he closed it behind them. He saw the marks where she landed on the ground, but only one set of prints led away.

Michael must have carried her. How curious. Jackson ran the possible reasons through his mind, but was stumped. It was a good sign, however. She was likely still alive and that gave him time to recover her before the leader of the dark pack could use the innocent girl for whatever purpose he had designed.

The tiny hairs on the back of his neck rose at the same moment a warning shiver flew up his spine. He crouched in the shadows, animal instincts taking over. He suppressed the overwhelming urge to change when he caught two glowing eyes moving through the base of trees at the edge of the yard. They didn't advance into the open, but it wasn't long before the scout was joined by another. Soon a full group paced back and forth, either sensing him or watching the broken window, which was the best access point into the human dwelling.

He was so focused on the distraction inside the forest he didn't hear the commotion out front before it was too late. A loud crash echoed off the trees, followed by a strange popping noise. Jackson realized the stalker's ruse had succeeded as he rose off the ground to his full height.

Jackson rounded the corner in a matter of seconds, but the trespassers were already gone. Their handiwork remained, however, and the warning they left behind was clear. The tires on the 4 wheel drive were slashed to ribbons, disabling the only chance they thought he had to escape with the women. Even if the rangers kept an additional set of snow tires for the winter, which was common, the windshield was kicked in and snow cascaded inside the empty vehicle.

For the first time in his life Jackson felt the fear of mortal danger. Not for himself, but for Jessica who was an innocent. He never believed Michael would so blatantly cross him, but Michael was no longer here and his little band of followers were far more dangerous on their own than he had ever imagined.

He had to get Jessica to safety and they needed to leave now. That last strike was the only warning he'd get before the rest of the pack came in on them. The thought of retreat left a bad taste in his mouth. His feral instincts urged him to defend his territory. He was furious at their lack of respect, their wild abandon for betrayal. But there was a time and place for retribution. And that time wasn't when Jessica's life was at risk.

He bounded onto the porch, bypassing all the steps before turning to make sure it was safe for her to open the door. "It's Jackson. Let me inside." He could hear her turning the lock before his sentence was complete. He slipped through and secured the door behind them.

•

Waiting for Jackson was one of the hardest things Jessica had ever done in her life. She felt blind inside the cabin, knowing she should stay away from the windows after what happened to Lucy.

"I hope he doesn't think I'm just going to sit here on my hands and do nothing while he goes out and saves my best friend," Jessica said out loud in the kitchen and the determination in her voice gave her a little bit of resolve.

She had rummaged through the drawers in search of a phone earlier, though at the time it didn't occur to her she might need a weapon. She draped Lucy's coat over the kitchen chair again, her hand lingering a little on the soft material before she returned to her search.

There has to be a hunting knife here somewhere. God, even an ice pick or a pizza cutter!

She was about to give up when she saw the overhead light glint off a set of keys shoved all the way to the back of the last drawer. One of the larger keys had the Ford logo stamped clearly on the end, and she remembered the truck out front under a foot of snow. It probably didn't matter. They could leave in whatever vehicle Jackson had brought.

Still, it was better than nothing so she decided to pocket the jangling mess when a loud thud hit the roof over the living room and landed with a terrible crash of glass and metal in the front yard. She stifled a cry at the unexpected sound. With her hand clamped firmly over her mouth she ran to the front door and placed her fingers on the bolt.

Don't turn it, don't turn it, she said to herself, making the phrase a calming mantra. Jackson told her not to open the door unless it was for him and she was going to wait at least ten whole seconds before she decided to go help. Jessica didn't realize she was holding her breath until she heard his muffled voice through the wooden door. As soon as he swept through the frame she started to ask him what he found, but the look on his face silenced her question.

"Listen to me carefully." He took both her hands in his until she looked him in the eye. "We need to leave here right now. I'll explain all of this later, but we don't have time for anything else."

"We have to take your car," she said in a steady voice. She pulled her hands away from him so he wouldn't notice she was shaking. "Our rental is stuck in a ditch down the road and it's not getting out anytime soon."

"I came here on foot," he said abruptly, and though she waited for his explanation as to how that was even possible, none was forthcoming. "However, we have other transportation."

"You mean the truck out front, right? I found the keys when you were outside." Her hands dug in the deep pockets of her coat for the metal ring, but before she could produce them he placed a finger on his lips. She watched as his entire body settled into a perfect stillness.

His eyes narrowed as he looked over her shoulder to the open bedroom. It was like something out of a horror movie, the absolute feeling of cold dread that washed over her entire body when she realized Jackson was watching something behind her back.

"Take my hand again." He reached forward so slowly she was afraid to move. "When I say ready, I want you to run out the front door just one step ahead of me. Do not turn around for anything."

"Oh, I can't forget Lucy's coat though. She'll need it." Jessica replied automatically as her mind numbly put the thought into her head through the shock. He held tight to her fingers but it didn't stop her from turning.

She saw the predatory eyes through the shattered windowsill in the bedroom, glowing red from the flickering flame she had stoked just a short time ago. Small shards of leftover glass tinkled softly onto the carpet from the window pane as two huge paws slid across the bottom of the frame, long claws scraping on the wood for purchase.

With a guttural growl the animal sprang forward, landing half way through the windowsill where a jagged shard of glass remained.

The massive form of the wolf writhed in pain and cried out in agony as the sliver sliced the underside of its soft belly. Thrashing wildly the creature fell back into the darkness and Jessica was able to hear the thud as it landed on the frozen ground.

"Ready," Jackson said clearly, but even though she heard him she couldn't make her legs move. Her face was numb and everything around them felt surreal as he wrapped his arm around her.

He held her to his side and they moved forward fluidly, her weight against him not the least bit of a deterrent. She saw a small outbuilding in the moonlight at the edge of the trees and realized he was leading them there. He set her up against the wall next to a small ramp while he entered some kind of code into the lock. His fingers flew so fast she couldn't have made out the numbers if she wanted to.

Once they were inside the temporary refuge it was completely silent. Jessica wanted to say something, do something, but she didn't know how she could help. If it hadn't been for Jackson she had no idea what might have happened to her tonight. For that matter, if she hadn't agreed to this trip then Lucy would be home in bed with a bottle of Nyquil watching *The Last Unicorn* for the twentieth time.

"You're doing fine, Jessica." Jackson seemed to know her thoughts as he crossed the small space between them. "I need you stay with me, okay? I want you to stay with me."

He added the last bit so quietly she wondered if she had heard it at all. The blood felt like it was flowing back into her extremities and she could stand on her own two legs again. She nodded as she looked into his beautiful brown eyes, so dark and full of mystery. Jessica barely knew this man and yet she trusted him completely. And why shouldn't she? All he'd done since the day she met him was keep her safe.

"I just need you to ... well, take off your clothes." The corners of his mouth turned up slightly, but as hard as she tried she couldn't see anything but seriousness in his eyes.

"Wait just a minute, buddy." She put her hands on her hips and tapped her foot sharply on the cement floor. "You save me from one wolf and you think I'm going to give you the treat of a lifetime? You should be so lucky!"

"Nine wolves" she could have sworn she heard him say under

his breath, but it was difficult to tell because he had turned his back to her. When he faced her again he was smiling.

"I need you to put on this snow suit and parka." He handed the down-filled set to her slowly so she had time to understand. "If you're cold now, you'll freeze to death on the ride and I promised myself I wouldn't let you die—tonight."

"Oh my gosh." Jessica blushed from her cheeks down to her toes. "I'm sorry I'm such a dork. I didn't mean to be rude."

"No worries," he answered her nonchalantly as he pulled the tarp off a gleaming ATV outfitted with snow tracks and primed it to start.

Jessica struggled into her cold weather gear as quickly as she could while he prepped the vehicle. She hadn't exactly donned sexy lingerie for the plane ride. After she was ready he tossed her a helmet and positioned himself at the front of the four-wheeler. When he turned to see what she was doing, she walked over to the rumbling ATV and slid one long leg across the back until she came to rest against him.

Jessica had butterflies in her stomach as the front of her body melded against him and she secured her arms low around his waist. She could feel his muscular legs flex against the inside of her thighs through all her clothing and had to force her hands to remain intertwined against his abdomen when she really wanted to touch his chest.

When he gunned the throttle she thought she felt a low, audible response vibrate though his body. He slipped one hand free and ran it over her calf pressed up against the machine. She supposed he wanted to make sure she was seated properly.

Jackson pulled a remote control from the pocket of his sleek leather jacket and hit a button that opened the door to the building. When the gap widened enough for them to exit, he surprised her by leaning back instead of forward, so he could speak.

"Out of curiosity—" He revved the engine, sending a jolt through her body. "How many wolves would I have to protect you from for you to take your clothes off?"

Chapter 11

Jessica had no idea how Jackson could see anything as they barreled along the trail through the woods. Even with the moonlight above the trees it was abysmally dark beneath the heavy foliage. Though it felt to her like they were careening at breakneck speed he seemed to know the way without the slightest hesitation. She was forced to trust him with her safety once again as she laid her head against his back.

Jackson freed one hand from the steering column at her movement, running his gloved fingers along the outside of her left leg where he tucked them underneath the bottom of her thigh against the seat.

She knew she should be shivering with the cold air whipping all around them. She couldn't even look ahead without the wind biting the small amount of skin exposed on her face, after all. But when Jackson touched her like that, with such familiar intimacy, she felt flames rush through her veins like her blood was on fire. She hoped he couldn't feel her telltale heart hammering away.

Jessica wanted to overstep her bounds. She wanted to be with Jackson more than anything she could ever remember wanting in her life, but she couldn't discount the way it would make Emily feel. Her heart told her that Jackson didn't belong with her friend. She might be naïve regarding the Hart family and what they were about, but she truly didn't think the sparks that flew between them at the ranger station could have happened if Jackson was Emily's man.

They'd been riding for a very long time, though she couldn't be sure of the distance, when she felt like Jackson was going easier along the trail. Whatever had attacked them back at the cabin must be far behind, but she felt a pang of fear when she realized Lucy was as well.

The ATV slipped a little as they climbed a steep incline and Jessica knew she had to relax and go with the flow. If she leaned the other way to balance herself out, it might flip the four-wheeler and they could end up in more danger than her missing friend.

She breathed a sigh of relief when they crested the top of a ridge, but that breath caught in her throat when she got her first glimpse of the Hart family hunting lodge. The sheer size of the mansion itself was impressive, as was the incredible granite and marble stone façade. Wrought iron and hardwood framework made up the bones of the ancient estate, laid out in dazzling patterns to support the design.

The soft, yellow glow of lights shone from a handful of windows on the south side of the property. Jessica felt a moment of apprehension as she wondered how welcoming they would actually be for her. The last time she had occasion to visit the Hart family she was thrown out almost as soon as she'd gotten there.

Jackson must have sensed her reticence because he covered her clenched hands with one of his own as they neared the intimidating structure. Her fingers tightened despite her resolve to stay calm and Jackson let the ATV idle to a stop several yards from the back courtyard. She could see the stone wall all the way around the rear entrance, broken up by black iron rods of fencing with sharp spikes on the end.

"This is my house and you will be welcome here. There is nothing to be afraid of as long as you remain on the grounds and under my protection." Jackson easily dismounted and stood at her side, one long leg propped up on the runner next to her frozen boot.

"I don't know. This all seems so crazy," she said through the small opening the hooded parka afforded her. "I mean, obviously something is wrong here—a lot of something, to be honest. But beside that, I know you're going to drop me off in that house with your people. If I recall, they aren't big fans of mine. I kind of get the feeling they'd eat me alive if they get the chance."

"Actually, that's not even funny." Jackson frowned and lowered the ice cold zipper below her chin. He pulled the glove off his right hand and gently lifted her chin until her eyes met his.

The butterflies started up again and Jessica couldn't help but be swayed by the look of desire that Jackson took no care to hide. His eyes strayed to her mouth and her lips parted on their own accord when he ran his thumb across her cheek.

Before she knew what she was doing, Jessica turned her face into the palm of his hand and pressed a kiss against his skin, feeling the deep life lines that ran across it. She knew the truth then, that she had to share a part of her life with Jackson no matter what she had to do or where it might take her. Jessica felt like she had come home for the first time in her life, standing in the middle of a snowy field on the mountain. She had always thought love was complicated, a constant trial of loyalty, disappointment and hard-won gains. It wasn't true at all. Nothing could be more simple and beautiful than the way she felt with her face cradled in the palm of Jackson's hand.

He leaned in and pulled her hood back. She thought he was going to kiss her as his right hand left her chin and slipped around the back of her neck, easily holding her and exposing her face to him at the same time. She could barely breathe as he lightly grazed her lips with his own, wanting to feel the pressure of his deep kiss.

She stared into his stormy brown eyes, his mouth hovering over hers just a fraction of an inch away. Jessica tried to push forward. She couldn't be that close and not touch him, but he held her immobile.

"You are driving me crazy, woman." He deliberately let the words out slowly, so that each hot breath fell on her sensitive skin when he spoke.

He didn't engage her with a kiss, but instead placed his mouth on her chin where his fingers had been just a short time ago. Jackson ran his hot lips along her jaw and stopped just below her ear where he lingered with a slight amount of pressure.

A wild shiver shot from her toes up through the top of her head. The effect was so disorienting that if she'd been standing her knees would have surely given out. Jackson turned his cheek against her neck and buried his face in her exposed skin as his teeth lightly grazed her pulse point.

Jessica got the unusual feeling he was tasting her, though she didn't mind at all. The thrill of being captured and held so completely by this powerful male, and yet so tenderly treated despite the urgency of their passion, was unlike anything she'd experienced before.

"We must get inside before this goes too far." Jackson's voice was rough with desire as he reluctantly pulled out of the embrace. She was too stunned to respond for a moment. This was clearly not what either of them wanted, yet he broke apart from her and turned his face so she couldn't see his emotions.

"Well, can it go too far once we're in the house?"

"Has anyone ever told you you're relentless?" Jackson faced her now with a smile he couldn't suppress.

"Funny you should say that. Relentless is my middle name."

"How odd," Jackson said with a perplexing tone as he swung back into the driver's seat. "I thought it would be something more regal, like Hopelessly Lost."

"I wasn't lost! Luckily I found you, didn't I?"

Jessica quickly pulled her hood back up as he started the engine, poking him in the side as she wrapped her arms around his waist. "No, I found you," Jackson commented over his shoulder as he slowly accelerated. "But I don't know how lucky you are."

Jessica had been teasing him with light-hearted banter to hide her true unease as they approached the lodge, but when he stopped at the heavily fortified rear gate she found she wasn't in such a jovial mood after all.

Her legs were painfully stiff as she swung them off the side of the vehicle. She noticed there was yet another key pad built into the stone by the massive gate, but once he entered the proper set of numbers a much smaller door opened to the left of the iron doors. She never would have noticed it if Jackson hadn't activated it.

They entered a beautiful garden of topiaries and secluded pathways, each illuminated by a small set of lights along the edges. Most everything was covered in snow, but she could see sculptures and emptied fountains in alcoves off to the sides and thought the place must be amazing in the summer.

They neared the back door and by the look of things through the brightly lit windows, they would be entering through the kitchen. That suited Jessica just fine. If she did have any luck at all, no one from the family would be up in the middle of the night raiding the fridge.

Jessica heard the strange sound just a moment after Jackson

had. He froze in mid-stride and his hand closed tightly over her fingers. The pressure was painful, but before she could say anything he put a finger to her lips.

At first she thought it was an animal, maybe a puppy that had gotten hurt and crawled into the bushes by the back door. Her heart wrenched at the pitiful cry the thing emitted and she moved forward out of instinct to help the creature.

"Don't, Jessica." Jackson held her back while he proceeded ahead, but he couldn't stop her from coming along. He could only keep her behind him.

"Oh my gosh, Jackson!" Jessica gasped when she saw the pale naked foot of a young woman between the steps and the greenery under the kitchen windowsill. "Is it Lucy? Let me see her!"

Jackson released her hand. Jessica told herself that he wouldn't have done it if there'd been any danger to her so she fell to her knees and crawled toward the woman in the bushes. Her beautifully shaped legs were scratched and muddy with decaying leaves and god knew what else plastered to her cold skin.

Jessica realized with hot cheeks the woman was completely naked, though she was so covered in muck that it was difficult to see much. Jackson stood just a few feet away and though he was speaking loudly into the intercom at the door, his words didn't penetrate the shock she was in.

"Go away!" the battered woman cried out and curled tighter into a fetal position.

Jessica almost tore her coat apart in an effort to remove it so she could cover the naked figure that strained to get away from her.

"No, it's okay. You're safe now. You don't have to run from me."

As Jessica tucked the white down filled parka around the huddling woman she noticed a lot of blood had stained the snow all around her. In fact, she was kneeling in it as she tried to make out the woman's face through the matted, stained hair.

"Leave me alone, Jessica!" the woman shrieked, slapping away her hands as she abruptly stood up against the stone wall beneath the window.

The parka fell away for a moment before Jackson sprang over the steps. He swiftly covered her again as several family members rushed through the door to take her inside, but not before Jessica saw the jagged gash on Emily's belly.

Chapter 12

"Jessica's presence is this house is extremely volatile," Meredith crossed the room of the great hall to face Jackson. "You have even more on your plate now and quite frankly I have no sympathy for you. She is a human female!"

"I know who she is," he answered his mother with a feral growl that raised the hackles on the back of his neck. He was in no mood to hear her disapproval.

"Then why did you bring her here? This puts the family in danger. I could see why you saved Emily; her situation was indirectly our problem. But this is unacceptable."

"What is unacceptable, Mother? Danger in this family is par for the course, so I must assume you object to my feelings for Jessica."

"So you admit you're throwing your life away for a less than desirable mate? You will bring shame to us all and lose everything your grandfather and father worked so hard to build for our people!" Meredith rarely allowed her voice to rise during an argument, but at the end of her admonishment she was almost shouting.

"I doubt I need to ask because I'm sure you're going to tell me, but how will my feelings for Jessica destroy their work?"

"You don't remember the war and bloodshed before your grandfather brought the bloodline together under the Hart family banner. As we fought each other, the old world hunters picked us off easily until our kind was nearly extinct. He brought this family to the new continent and founded these safe ranges for us to hunt in. If we don't mend the breach created by Michael it will happen all over again."

"I ask you once more, what does that have to do with my feelings for Jessica?"

Meredith approached him and laid her hand on his shoulder. If he didn't know any better, he thought he could see sympathy in her eyes before she spoke.

"The only way to bring Michael back into the family would be for you to take one of his females as your mate. He can't choose within our clan. His bloodline is too close. Had he grown up normally we would have found him a bride from a distant clan as we should have done for you. It's up to you to heal these wounds and bring them back into the fold. You can't be with Jessica. She's not our kind and you don't know what could happen. If the Patriarch breaks the rules, they will no longer apply to any of us. It's terribly risky!"

Jackson's heart ached with his mother's words. He couldn't deny his duty as leader of the pack. He would never know Jessica's love and the thought tortured him. He would see their guest and her friend safe before he committed to anything. Even if he had just a few precious days with the beautiful woman, the memories of it would have to last him a lifetime.

Meredith patted him in a conciliatory manner, but he shrugged her hand away. Perhaps she was right in her assessment, but for the wrong reasons. Any kind of life Jessica might have with him would be fraught with danger and intrigue. She would be forced to leave her loved ones behind and even if she agreed to all of that, he wasn't permitted to change her. She would live out a mortal life among those who would always judge her for being different.

Jackson heard the sound of frantic footfalls before they came near the grand hall. Roland cantered around the corner and through the foyer. The scent of fear and confusion hung heavily about the young man, which put Jackson on alert.

Meredith quickly moved to join his side, ready to stand with him if need be, despite their disagreement—that was what made them family and it was the bond they all shared. Jackson couldn't allow that bond to falter.

"It's Emily. She left me a note. I swear I was only away from her bedside for a minute! I have no idea when she found the time to write this."

With an overwhelming feeling of foreboding, Jackson took the parchment from Roland's shaking hand and held it up to the light. Meredith began to read it at the same time, though she quickly turned away wearing an expression of distaste. He continued to read the note.

My Dear Roland,

There are so many things I'm sorry for since we first met, more than I could list at the moment. You watch me so carefully I barely have time to write this for you. Let me just say I didn't understand what happened at first, or how you saved me. I never meant to hurt you and now, as I tell you these things, I wonder how it took me so long to realize I love you with all of my heart.

I don't know if Jackson has told you yet that I was the one at the cabin last night, but it's not what he thinks. God, what you all must think ... I knew Michael would come for Lucy and I wanted to keep her safe. I was too late to stop him, but not too late for the beating I received from the Dark Breeders after my wound weakened me. They called me a traitor when they caught me at the cabin. They said they turned me and I abandoned them when they needed me most.

I do not believe that. I think they left me to die, which I would have done if you hadn't given me your breath of life. I can't allow the same thing to happen to Lucy, I won't leave her in their hands. Forever and always ...

Emily

Reading those words of loyalty wrenched Jackson's heart even more. In a way, they shared a bond like that of the Hart family clan. He had no doubt losing one member of the trio would devastate the remaining two. If he had his way they'd never have to experience such a loss.

The thought of what Michael could be doing to her friend must have driven Emily right off her sick bed and into imminent danger despite the terrible injuries she received the night before. She was a strong woman, worthy of Roland, and he was pleased that he was not wrong about their match.

"I imagine you'll be leaving at once to retrieve both girls," Meredith said dispassionately. Perhaps she knew in advance any argument against it would fall flat and wisely decided to go along with the idea. Or perhaps she had a heart after all. She had never been a soft woman, but Jackson always thought there was a bit of compassion to the manner in which she took Emily in.

"She's wounded, Jackson," Roland reminded him with urgency. "Emily can't fight Michael by herself and I have no doubt she'd do exactly that if she thought it would protect Lucy. She probably wouldn't even be able to shift."

"She'll have a big head start, I'm afraid. I couldn't be sure she was at the cabin last evening, but I suspected the rogue Dark Breed was Emily. She'll have the trail long before either of us."

"She may have been infected by them, but she is not one of those uncivilized brutes, do you hear me?" Roland turned on Jackson with a snarl.

"I meant no disrespect, Roland." Jackson spoke his apology sincerely. He did his best to ignore the look of disdain in Meredith's eyes as she watched her son give ground to a less dominate male. "We'll make this right, all of it, and I will not stop until everyone is safe within the family."

"I believe you. As always, I defer to your judgment." Roland tipped his head to the side with a submissive acknowledgement. Jackson nodded to his mother to ensure she understood the fact he still had the upper hand. He was learning his own way to lead the clan and every situation he resolved enabled him to grow into the role with more respect from the others.

•

The trail at the cabin was cold. No one had been back to the location since the incident that evening, which told Jackson they got what they came for. There was never any rhyme or reason to the Dark Breed attacks, at least none he could figure, so he hoped they wouldn't make a try for Jessica.

Woe be to any of the feral clan who dared lay a finger on that woman. There wouldn't be enough pieces for them to identify.

He instructed Roland to leave the ATVs in the shed so they could go forward on foot. He knew Michael had carried Lucy in his human form; he wouldn't have been able to shift with the captured female. Their trail should be easy enough to follow.

It wasn't that he was concerned about finding them. He knew he would eventually. Time was his biggest concern in the end.

Michael had had her for a day now and he was capable of anything they could imagine—and some things he didn't dare.

Roland exchanged perplexed glances with him as they walked along the edges of the trail. It was almost too easy to follow their progress. Could it be an ambush? Michael was never this careless. Even more curiously, no other prints followed those of the Dark Breed leader. Whatever those renegade wolves were doing back at the ranger station, they went their separate way from Michael.

The trees grew thick up ahead and his brother must have struggled through the branches, but he never appeared to set Lucy down on the ground. Jackson caught the scent of a wood fire in the area, fresh and still smoking. Perhaps he set up camp in a clearing nearby when he felt it was safe.

They weren't able to stay off the path any longer as the passage between the trees was incredibly narrow, so they set their boots on top of the footsteps they followed. No one had done anything to hide them, so Jackson didn't think they'd lose the trail soon.

They finally broke free of the forest and found themselves standing in an open field. An ancient farmhouse sat at the top of the gentle slope, grey slats of wood warped and twisted on what must have been a beautiful home at one time. It wasn't unusual to come across an old homestead or two while crossing the vast expanse of their private land. This was no abandoned house, however dilapidated it appeared. Smoke curled up into the grey sky from the brick chimney and the soft glow of candlelight filled one of the rooms on the upper level.

"Do you think they're inside? I don't catch any sign of Emily here." Roland turned an earnest face toward his pack leader. "If Michael has harmed her in any way, Jackson, I can't be responsible for what I will try to do to him. I need you to know that now."

Jackson nodded at the man, understanding his situation. His heart was torn and he really didn't know what he would do if Roland engaged his brother in a battle that would surely result in one of their deaths. He was responsible for the young man's protection, and Emily's, who was in his care. But he still loved his brother despite the things he'd done since their father's death.

I'll cross that bridge when I come to it, he thought to himself. *Just please don't let that bridge be on my path today.*

Both men were at the steps leading to the sloping veranda

and though no one could move more silently than Jackson, the boards creaked. He cringed, but after a moment of silence and no repercussions, he advanced.

The rusted coil on the screen door made a screeching sound when he opened it and he thought they might as well just knock and wait for Michael to answer at the rate they were going.

The front door was unlocked, much to his surprise. He pushed it inward, preparing himself for the cold, desolate conditions his brother would be treating Lucy to.

The interior of the house was nothing like he imagined.

He was amazed at how warm it was inside the drafty old homestead. He and Roland stood in the small foyer like two uncomfortable guests who knew they didn't belong. Jackson could see a welcoming fire in the sitting room through the open door on his left and carefully stepped toward the entryway.

The furnishings were threadbare, that much was apparent, but they were lovely with an antique charm one couldn't get at the local department store. Though he had no explanation for it, Jackson felt so much at home in the sitting room that it almost seemed familiar.

"You're not going to believe this," Roland spoke quietly from across the parlor, his voice full of surprise as he faced the country fireplace.

Jackson came to his side, his attention drawn to a row of picture frames along the mantle. They looked old, and many of the photos surely were antique with their black and white or sepia tones. But that wasn't what shook him to the very core of his being.

His hand flew to his mouth to cover a gasp when he saw the picture of his young parents, together and happy before his father had passed on. There was a light in his mother's eyes that he knew he hadn't seen since the day of the funeral. Just seeing the image of the man he loved so much in the frame before him brought back feelings he buried for far too long. It was all he could do to retain his composure when Roland picked up another picture in a dark wooden frame.

"Look at this one." He said it calmly, but his knuckles were white as he held it out.

Jackson took the photo and gazed at Michael and himself, laughing together as they both laid brushes to a mural on the wall in front of them. He suddenly remembered that day as if it had just happened, his brilliant brother telling him how easy it would be to paint everything they could dream of. Jackson didn't have the heart to tell him he wasn't gifted in the same way, so he did his best to make his part in the mural acceptable.

Michael had thrown his arms around his waist when they were through and told him it was the most beautiful, magical painting he'd ever seen. Jackson didn't wish to discourage the child who was such a dreamer, but he could see a clear difference between their works. In the end it hadn't mattered. The fact that he'd spent the afternoon with his younger brother meant more than anything else to the boy.

"Jackson," Roland whispered urgently, his voice painfully cutting through the memory forgotten for all those years. "I just heard movement upstairs!"

Chapter 13

Jackson was suddenly on alert. His emotions clouded his judgment and he needed to rein them in. Jackson couldn't afford to make any mistakes inside this house, not when he was so close to finding Jessica's friend.

The pair approached the staircase that rose to the second floor. After testing the wooden steps they ascended as quietly as possible, but Jackson knew they may as well have thundered up the stairwell with a herd of elephants in tow. Any sound they made, no matter how minor, would inform Michael if he was anywhere in the vicinity.

A small room stood open at the top of the stairs and he could see a clawfoot tub in the corner, clean and ready for use. That meant there was a well nearby and the water was still good. But why bring the girl here? What did this house mean to Michael?

They came to the next room and Jackson set his hand on the brass knob, testing to see if it was locked. The metal was surprisingly warm and he could see the soft glow of firelight from beneath the crack of the door, which swung inward, making no sound as the two men stepped inside. The fireplace was stoked and putting out a considerable amount of heat. Jackson was so surprised by the sight before him that he barely remembered to close the door so no one could surprise them.

Lucy was lying in a beautiful four-post bed covered with a white down comforter. She'd been dressed in an old-fashioned linen nightgown, the intricate lace cuffs and neckline yellowed with time. Her red hair cascaded over the white pillows, clean and brushed to a shine.

Jackson could hardly believe his eyes, but a crystal vase filled with fresh cut flowers sat nearby on the nightstand. There was a worn green velvet chair at the edge of the bed and Jackson could almost see the specter of his brother as he lingered in it, watching the girl sleep.

What is going on here? Is he playing house with Lucy? Jackson's mind raced through all the possibilities, but only one made sense after everything he had seen.

Lucy tossed fitfully in her sleep before settling again, making the same sound the two men heard when they were downstairs. Roland stood guard at the door while Jackson approached the girl. He laid a hand on her forehead; she was feverish. He remembered Jessica saying she was ill when they were back at the ranger station, but her condition had clearly worsened.

"Look at her, Jackson," Roland whispered from the doorway. "I can see it from here. He's turning her. And from the look of it, she was bitten a long time before they got here."

Oh God, could Roland be correct?

Now Jessica would lose both of her friends to the turning and he didn't know how he could possibly explain it. In fact, Jessica was probably the only person within a fifty miles radius who wasn't a shifter now. Everything was falling apart and he didn't know how to put it back together again.

"What should we do?" Roland looked to him from his position at the door and Jackson knew the young man was depending on him. He could see his mother's face in his mind's eye, reminding him everyone did. No pressure there.

Jackson had witnessed a few turnings in his lifetime. Lucy wasn't doing well at all. Michael must have known she was in danger of failing. Perhaps he'd even gone for help. Who knew?

"We have to get her back to the lodge right now. Once she's under the doctor's care we'll return to scout for Emily if she's not back there ahead of us."

Jackson carefully pulled the heavy comforter off the girl and picked her up with ease. He faltered for a moment when her eyelids fluttered and she murmured Michael's name.

His brother would surely be frantic when he returned and Lucy was gone. He didn't know how he could feel sympathy for the man who turned so many innocent people and left so many others to die. But he did.

Jackson realized he was still clutching the picture of himself with Michael when they were younger. He felt like he was laying down a part of his heart when he gently put the wooden frame face up on the bed as a message to his brother.

•

"I want to know what's going on with you people right now! At least let me see Emily."

Jessica was tired of playing nice. She could only take so many naps in the guest room before she started to feel confined. Jackson had been gone for an entire day and no one at the lodge felt inclined to enlighten her regarding his whereabouts, especially the attendant to the doctor who stood with his arms crossed in front of the door to the medical wing.

"Listen buddy," she jabbed her finger against his chest and it was like poking a brick wall. "I'm sure Jackson wouldn't be happy to hear you were rude to me when all I wanted to do was pay a visit to my friend."

"That's probably true." The massively built orderly frowned a little when she mentioned Jackson's name. She really thought she was on to something then because that was the first time she had gotten any reaction out of him.

Before she could explore that angle further the stubborn door guard raised his eyes and looked over her shoulder with interest. He cocked his head like he was listening for something, but she couldn't hear a thing down the corridor.

She turned around in time to see the commotion at the end of the hall. The moment she laid eyes on Jackson with the tiny figure in his arms she knew it was Lucy. But her friend wasn't moving. The way her arms and legs dangled listlessly through Jackson's grasp left her with terror in the pit of her stomach. She immediately fell in line behind Jackson with every intention of climbing over the orderly if she had to.

"Let her through, David." Jackson's tone left no room for misunderstanding.

"Doc told me she can't come inside."

"We can't keep the truth from her any longer."

Jessica felt awkward as he spoke about her like she wasn't even in the hall. It was clear this family had some pretty big secrets, but she couldn't image what might be so terrible they had to live by themselves in the middle of a forest on the edge of nowhere.

Were they gangsters, or a leper colony? Maybe they were aliens.

She had conjured up so many outrageous ideas in the absence of the truth that any information he divulged to her would probably be tame compared to her imagination. The important thing was that he decided to trust her. She was determined to show him no matter what the truth was, it wouldn't change her feelings for him.

And now that she was permitted inside she'd be able to be with her friend. The doctor worked fast, allowing Jessica to be in the room as long as she stayed out of the way. She sat on a hard plastic chair in the corner nervously twisting her hands.

"Does she have the same disease Emily has? Is it contagious?"

"I suppose she does in a way, young lady." The white-haired doctor peered at her over his spectacles, suddenly interested in her comment. "You've been with her constantly the last few days, haven't you?"

"Well, except for the last day. I tried, but she went missing. I never should have let her sleep in that room by herself."

"Has she seen anyone else since this began, any other doctors or medics?"

"Well, before we left, our family doctor gave her a rabies shot, but it was no big deal. We don't even think she had a bite or anything."

The moment she said those words the color drained from the doctor's face and he looked at Jackson with alarm.

"The shot they gave her will fight against the turning process. I've never seen it done. She very well may recover her humanity, but she'll be at high risk after. If Michael infects her again, she will die."

"Who the hell is Michael?" Jessica asked.

"She needs to leave now, and I think you'd better tell her everything, although I don't know what will happen after you do." The doctor nodded to Jackson with a sign of respect and turned back to his patient as they left.

"This is going to be good." Jessica stood in the outer hallway with the mysterious head of the Hart clan. She wanted to yell at him, demand explanations, but the look in his eye was so tormented she was afraid she'd somehow push him over the edge.

"The doctor said Lucy will recover, Jessica. It's everything we could hope for. I know all of this must seem crazy to you, but if you give me a chance I'll tell you everything later. I want you to know me, and to hell with the consequences."

"If you're honest with me, Jackson, no matter what the truth is, there's nothing we won't be able to overcome together." She wanted to reach out to him, touch him and somehow ease this terrible burden he carried.

"Could we have dinner in your room this evening? Roland needs me at once, but I'd like to have time alone with you to explain, if you find you can wait a little longer."

"Well, I'm not going anywhere apparently," she answered. She was stranded on a mountain with no roads leading in or out. Even if she had a map she wouldn't be able to find the ranger station again.

She wasn't afraid for herself, though. Jackson told her she would be safe here and it was the one thing she believed. As annoying as she'd been to everyone all day, they would have done something to her by now if they'd been allowed. The rest of her thoughts were a jumble of confusion and strange ideas.

"Do you have time to walk me back to my room?" The lodge was huge, but she had been all over it several times by now—at least in the places she was authorized. It wasn't that she couldn't find her way, but she wanted just a few more moments with Jackson before he left her again.

He took her hand and slid it inside the crook of his left arm, much like the evening he had escorted her through the estate at Hocking Hills. As they walked together on this night, he allowed his leg to brush against the outside of her thigh on occasion. Every time he touched her a feeling of electricity shot through her body.

When they reached her door she turned to face him, hoping for a kiss. Jackson hesitated for a moment, searching her eyes as if determining her state of mind. He leaned close, but instead of kissing her lips, he rested his cheek on her neck. Jackson firmly pressed his mouth against her pulse point where he must surely be able feel her hamming heart.

She wrapped her arms around his shoulders, wanting to pull herself close to him. The moment she pressed against his hard chest he bit her neck. It was a slight graze, not enough to break the skin, but her reaction was wild. Her legs turned to jelly and she could barely breathe.

Jackson had her through the door and on the bed before she knew what was happening. He was so strong and fast she barely noticed the transition. He straddled her below the waist, making no effort to hide his arousal for her as he ran his hands over her curves.

She moved with his touch, raising her hips against him with the rhythm of his caress. Jackson lifted his head to the ceiling and moaned with a terrible sense of frustration before he released her, his feet on the floor and away from the bed in a flash.

"You have no idea how hard this is for me." His voice was low and his eyes gleamed in the near darkness of the room.

"I think I have some idea," Jessica said. She looked him up and down with a sultry gaze that lingered near his waist. Every muscle on his body was taut and she could see him strain to exert control. She knew it was a terrible thing to do, tease him when he didn't have the time to follow through. But each encounter with him was more thrilling than the last and she couldn't find it in her heart to regret these stolen moments.

"I'll be back, Jessica." The tone of his voice let her know he was gravely serious. "And Heaven help you then, my dear."

•

He called me my dear, she thought with pleasure as she poured another glass of wine. Jackson hadn't been gone long when someone from the kitchen knocked on her door. One of the staff had been instructed to take her menu preferences for their dinner that night. She was struck by how thoroughly Jackson took care of her, even with everything else he had to worry about.

It was very late when they brought the tray up, but there was no sign of her date. Likely he told them to serve her if he was running behind. She wasn't interested in food, but didn't think she should neglect the wine selection that came with it.

The fire burned low and she strolled over to the hearth, sitting close while she put small logs on the coal bed. She had another glass while she enjoyed the warmth of the flames. She was afraid she'd doze off if she remained where she was, so she stood up a little wobbly on her feet. Earlier that day she noticed a set of double doors that lead to a small balcony off her room, but it was too cold to think about going out at that time.

Perhaps a bit of fresh air was exactly what she needed. By the look of things through the curtains, the moon was full and centered over the tree line in the distance. Silver light sparkled on the frozen snow, making the shadows from the tree tops look like spikes reaching out to her. It was so bright she could see almost as well as she could during a sunset.

A small amount of movement caught her eye at the edge of the forest and she squinted to make it out. Two distinct figures broke free from the shadows and sprinted toward the lodge. Jessica could clearly see it was some kind of animal. One of the creatures lagged behind from time to time and she thought maybe it was tired or hurt.

When they came closer Jessica decided they might be a cold weather breed of dog, a husky maybe. Or even wolves. Every time the smaller of the two lost ground, the lead animal doubled back and waited.

They were almost to the gate now and if she didn't know better she'd think they knew just what they were doing as they approached the large iron door. A light came on beneath her and a door had opened from the kitchen. Someone was coming through and they didn't know it wasn't safe outside.

She nearly called out to the unsuspecting newcomer. He was just below her balcony, but her words stuck in her throat when she saw it was Jackson. He carried a heavy blanket in his arms as he hurried toward the back gate, which opened as he approached. There stood Emily. Jessica covered her mouth so she wouldn't make a sound, but it wasn't easy with her friend standing in the courtyard as naked as she was the other evening.

Jackson swiftly wrapped the blanket around her. She collapsed against him in a clumsy, tired way. He put his arm around her for support as he led her inside. And the remaining wolf followed both of them. All three went into the kitchen and quietly closed the door behind them.

What did I just see? I know I'm not stupid, but am I crazy?

Jessica walked over to the table in her room and picked up the bottle, looking for the alcohol percentage on the label. At any rate, she ought to go downstairs and find out what this was all about. She remembered her way to the kitchen fairly well, and though she didn't intend to sneak up on anyone, their conversation was so intense they still didn't notice her. What she saw inside that room shook her so badly her fingers loosened on the wine bottle she still carried; it crashed to the floor.

The last thing she saw before she instinctively ran was the look of dread on Jackson's face.

Chapter 14

Jackson sprinted back to the lodge ahead of Roland and Emily. He was acutely aware Jessica was waiting for him upstairs and might be thinking he didn't give a damn about her after all. Nothing would be further from the truth, but it couldn't be helped. He would have to trust her now as much as she'd have to trust him by the end of the evening.

He and Roland had discovered Emily on the west side of the lake, exhausted to the point she could hardly run. The girl had barely learned to shift, let alone control it, and she was injured to boot. Yet they found her miles away from the manor house.

He could clearly see what the three friends had in common. They were stubborn to a fault and never gave up on one another. It was an admirable quality, one he prized highly among his family members, too. He just couldn't imagine how Jessica would handle the truth about Emily—and the truth about him as well.

Jackson scouted ahead through the trees to secure their passage while Roland remained behind with his mate to pace her. She would lose control and change back once she reached her ultimate point of exhaustion. He didn't think that was far off.

Jackson didn't expect to see Jessica downstairs, yet he shifted just the same as he tore through the corridors. He was quick about the transformation, tossing on borrowed clothing. His hurried flight through the lodge drew the attention of his mother who followed him back through the kitchen. He didn't give her the chance to ask questions. He needed to meet Emily and Roland on the other side of the gate and take the girl inside before anyone saw them. Meredith was waiting when they came through.

"Whenever you're ready, I'd like to know what exactly is going on here." She paced in front of the antique cast iron stove in the corner. It had been many years since the beast of an oven had been used for cooking, but the housekeepers still lit wood in the belly of the stove as a nostalgic source of heat.

"It was Michael," Emily said, fading in and out of consciousness as she shivered inside the blanket Jackson put around her shoulders.

"Wake her up!" his mother demanded, her tone unusually shrill. Just the mention of that name set the woman on edge. "What did he do to you?"

Roland remained in his feral form and stalked close to Emily's side, perhaps preparing to defend her against the angry matriarch who towered over her in the chair.

"No, he didn't hurt me. He set me free."

Everyone in the room was surprised by the admission and Jackson stepped between his mother and the exhausted girl. He knew she must rest soon, but he had to learn more. Perhaps if Meredith wasn't hanging over her slumped form like a preying gargoyle he could get answers.

"You can tell me, Emily. I'm not angry at all. I only want to protect you ... all of you."

"I know you do, Jackson." She fixed her eyes on his and stared intently at him in an effort to focus. "But even you can't protect Jessica from yourself, can you?"

He lost his breath when she mentioned her friend's name. There was no malice in Emily's statement, just a simple understanding that only one who has also given her heart might comprehend.

Oh hell, even Emily knows I'm screwed, Jackson thought frantically. He couldn't afford to show this vulnerable side of his emotions right now, not with his brother on the loose.

"What do you mean, Michael let you go?"

"His pack, they caught me in a trap in the forest. They caged me." Her voice was thick with the horror of her experience. Only a wolf could ever know the torture that came from being locked away in a cell. "They kept me there all day, taunting me, wearing me down. I couldn't rest for a moment before they started in on me again."

Everyone present shuddered at the thought of what she had gone through. Even Meredith gazed sympathetically at the girl and reached out a gentle hand to stroke her tangled hair in comfort.

"Michael came upon us, and he was furious when he saw me. I thought he would kill me then, but I wasn't the one he was mad at. He called the pack uncivilized and said they'd gone too far. He ordered them to release me and then asked me to bring you a message, Jackson."

"He knows I have Lucy, then?" All eyes fell on Jackson and he noticed Meredith unconsciously set her hand against the base of her own throat.

"He does know. He asked me to bid you to take care of her, please."

It was true then. Michael had feelings for Lucy after all. Jackson hadn't thought him capable after the past few years of debauchery. What else had he been wrong about?

"He asked for one more thing." Emily hesitated and her eyes shifted nervously to Meredith before they settled back on Jackson. "He wanted you to come back and see him at the old homestead. Michael said if you came alone he would tell you a secret. And then your mother would be forced to tell you the truth."

Everyone in the room was silent over the implications, but no one dared meet Meredith's eyes except Jackson. He was alarmed by her sudden pallor, and by the telltale way her fingers twisted the elegant strand of pearls at her neck. She was never the kind of woman to fidget or show weakness.

"Is there something you need to say to me?" His attempt to question her fell flat as she turned her face away from his searching eyes.

"I don't think you should go alone," Roland said from his place next to Emily. Jackson had been so distracted by his mother he didn't see Roland transform. "If you decide, that's your course. However, I'll go to the ranger station and make sure everything is... tidy."

Jackson was about to thank him for offering to take care of that dangerous loose end, when the sound of heavy glass shattered on the tile just outside the kitchen doorway. He spun around in the blink of an eye and caught Jessica, frozen in the shadows. Though it only lasted a second, the look of disbelief on her face was burned forever in his memory.

Damn it all, what had she seen?

•

Jessica didn't bother to look over her shoulder as she sprinted through the corridors that led away from the kitchen. She knew any one of the people in that room could be on top of her right now if they wanted to be.

Am I sure about what I saw?

Jessica slowed her pace when she realized no one was following at her heels. She needed to see Lucy right away, and if at all possible, get her out of this place if she was well enough to move.

Roland had been partially behind the counter, she thought to herself, her mind already making excuses. When she attempted to recall the memory of the shocking transformation Emily's husband had made, she suddenly found she couldn't.

He did not turn from a wolf into a man in the middle of the kitchen like it was nothing. I can't even remember seeing it now. Just let me make sure Lucy is alright before I face Jackson.

"Let's face it, girlie," she sarcastically counseled herself as she neared the medical wing. "He's probably a werewolf, or you're a lunatic. Either way you'd have to sleep in separate beds every time the full moon came around."

The door was slightly open where David usually stood and a feeling of vulnerability washed over her. She was by herself in a house full of God only knew what type of creature. The one thing she'd come to count on in the last day or two was Mr. Brick Wall would be standing in front of that door ready to give her a hard time.

Jessica didn't make a sound as she pushed the door open and slipped inside the outer office. The door to Lucy's room was open a little, too. That settled it then. David was inside with the doctor, just checking on the girl. She relaxed and stepped forward when she heard the elder man's deep voice in the open room.

"Don't do this, Michael. Why would you want to hurt such a sweet and kind young woman? I don't understand what you've become, my dear boy."

Michael! It was the same person who had taken Lucy from the ranger station at the outskirts of the preserve. Now she could finally see who was doing this to her friend.

"Hurt her?" The intruder responded as she crept close to the crack in the door and his voice struck her as familiar. "I don't wish to hurt her, old man. I want to love her."

Jessica covered her mouth as she caught a glimpse of the villain who stood at Lucy's bedside—the same dangerously handsome man they'd discovered at the manor house in Hocking Hills! It all came flooding back to her in an instant—the way he'd taken to Lucy. He'd kissed her hand and promised he'd see her again.

Had he bitten her then? Their family physician was sure she had a puncture wound from a canine.

"I don't think you understand, young one." The doctor's voice was so compassionate toward the intruder that she was confused by his response.

"She can't turn anymore. She will always be human from this day forward, but if you infect her once more, even accidentally, she won't be able to fight it off again. She will surely die and every time you come into contact with her you take that chance."

"What can you do to help her, Reginald?" He turned to face the physician and Jessica saw tears in the man's eyes.

"The only solution would be to sever all ties with her. Never see her again."

"I can't do that. Please don't ask that of me. What can you do to help me, then?"

"You don't know what you're asking, Michael," the doctor whispered in disbelief, turning away from the dark and brooding youngster who remained at Lucy's bedside.

"I know more than you think. More than any of you ever decided to give me credit for!" He swung around defiantly, eyes glowering at the old man in the corner. With no warning whatsoever, he moved his gaze slowly until he met Jessica's eyes peering at him through the crack in the door.

"That's right, Jessica," his voice was low, with that smooth and melodic tone again. "Come inside. I think you've learned enough at the door. I let you linger because you deserve answers, the same as I do."

She looked at Reginald in panic and he gestured for her to enter. If she didn't know what to believe before, the scene she just witnessed didn't lend her clarity. She wanted to hate Michael, and probably did on some level. But no matter what she could and couldn't understand that day, she wasn't able to deny that Michael was in love with Lucy. The emotion was all over his face.

"Remind my brother I await him at the old homestead." He held her gaze earnestly, waiting to see if she understood his message.

Jessica had no idea who he meant and was afraid her ignorance would be dangerous for them all. Before she was forced to admit it, the doctor stepped forward.

"I'm sorry, Michael. He hasn't told her who you are."

"I'm one more secret hidden by the family legacy, I see." The leader of the Dark Breed clan moved back to Lucy, gingerly taking her limp hand in own. Jessica thought he was kissing her bare skin, but she realized his lips remained a miniscule amount above her pallid flesh, not quite making contact.

"At least I was honest with Lucy." He turned his liquid black eyes toward her, catching her gaze. "It's more than I can say Jackson has done for you."

Michael stood up then. With stiff movements he unbuttoned his shirt. Jessica had no idea what he was doing, but the resident doctor became alarmed.

"Don't do this, Michael, please. Not in front of her."

The rogue took a step toward her and unbuttoned his pants. She couldn't even panic as he shrugged his shirt off his shoulders.

"Just so there's no room left in your mind for doubt, my dear Jessica." He drawled languidly, taking one more step. He stretched in a leisurely manner and as she watched him he crouched low to the ground. He didn't writhe in pain, not like she'd seen in the movies. The transformation was elegant and fluid as the man before her became the wolf he was in a handful of seconds.

The change was so natural Jessica wondered for a moment what could possibly be wrong with anything so beautiful. That was until the wolf sprang for her, easily knocking her down to the floor as he planted his heavy paws on her chest.

"If you bite her, Michael, I will kill you without hesitation." There was nothing in the doctor's tone that left anything to doubt on that account.

Jessica braced herself for the worst, but instead of teeth she felt a warm, wet tongue slide across her cheek before the massive creature sprung away. Oh for heaven's sake, he was playing with her!

Michael was gone so quickly her eyes didn't catch his exit. She decided to remain on the cold tiles just a bit longer in case there were any more surprises on the way. "Is there anything else I need to know?" she asked from her position on the floor. From the look on the doctor's face there probably was, but he sure wasn't going to be the one to tell her.

Chapter 15

"Dinner's cold," Jessica said, not willing to meet Jackson's eyes at the moment. "I'm probably going to need another bottle of wine, too—or five."

She hadn't been waiting long in her room for the leader of the Hart clan, but the short amount of time she spent there alone allowed for some of the shock to wear off.

She'd always been a sensible girl, even prided herself on her reputation for stability. Now everything was off-kilter and she was surprised to discover she was very emotional when he finally got there.

"Jessica, I don't even know where to begin. I should have told you sooner, I know that. But somehow I convinced myself I was protecting you by keeping the truth just another day longer." Jackson advanced slowly and she noticed he kept his hands in his pockets as he faced her.

It reminded her so much of the day they met when she impulsively hugged him outside of the mall. She'd never experienced anything like the feeling that gripped her entire being in that one single moment when he put his arms around her for the first time.

"Please, look at me." He freed one hand to lift her chin. She couldn't tear herself away from his gaze once he held it. His eyes were such a warm and rich shade of brown. He couldn't hide his distress as he carefully measured her reaction to his touch.

"You're one of them, aren't you?" It wasn't really a question. "What am I saying? You're the King of them. What does that make me? Because I sure don't fit in to your world."

"You are my world, Jessica. You're always on my mind no matter how much I try to banish the constant thought of you." He didn't try to stop her as she pulled away, and she was glad because she didn't want him to see the tears she was struggling to suppress.

"Somehow I don't think your family will approve. Meredith is your mom, right? I could tell right away, you know, because she didn't like me."

"I don't think she approves of anyone, to be honest—especially me. I haven't exactly conformed to her idea of a family leader." Jackson looked away from her then, and she knew there was something he didn't want her to see in his eyes when he spoke about his family responsibilities.

Of course, she thought to herself. He has no wife. Even I wondered about that when we first met. And now I know that can never be me.

"So, you were just going to play with me until it came time to get serious and settle down with someone you didn't have to keep secret? Lucky for you Emily came with so many single friends, eh?"

"No, Jessica." He took her by the shoulders and pulled her close. "I would never dishonor you that way. I tried to keep you at arm's length at first, because you are so different from anyone I've ever known. I'm acutely aware of how extraordinary you are. So beautiful and strong." His words faded away as he lowered his voice to a whisper. "From the first moment I saw you I wanted to kiss you more than anything I'd ever wanted in my life. It was for that very reason I didn't touch you right away when you put your arms around me. I knew I'd never be able to stop, and I was right."

His confession broke away the last of her reservations and she suddenly didn't care if she had him for one day or one lifetime. All she needed was now. Jessica wanted to share all she was with him, to open up her heart and wrap the whole of her being around his body. Even once could last forever in her memory.

His mouth was suddenly on hers, gentle at first, but as she pressed back, he gave her the full force of his ardor. Jessica could barely breathe he held her so tightly against his chest. She could feel the heat from his skin through their clothes. She tangled her fingers through his long, thick hair with a valiant effort to hold on as she slid her right leg between his thighs and pressed her hip against him.

She gasped as she felt the full force of his arousal pulse against her body. Jessica released her right hand and ran her fingertips across the small of his back, nails grazing his blazing skin before she palmed the back of his thigh, crushing him against her.

"Oh, God!" Jackson staggered backward, nearly falling over his own feet to get away from her. "I can't do this to you. I won't."

"No, it's okay. Really you can. I don't mind." She answered him urgently, confused by his reaction to her advances.

"You don't understand, Jessica. Wolves mate for life."

"Oh. And I'm not a wolf." The sudden implication hit her, something she hadn't even considered up until that point. What could happen if they got together? Would he be bound to her for the rest of his life? Maybe he was trying to protect her from that.

"Would you have me, Jessica? If I found a way to leave all this behind, could you accept me as I am?"

Her heart wrenched painfully when he said those words to her. She saw vulnerability in his eyes that had never been there before and knew she couldn't let that become a part of who he was.

Yes, yes! I'll take you! Her mind screamed the silent words inside her brain. *We'll run away from all this. I don't care about anything other than being with you!*

It wasn't true, though. She did care about something else. She cared about Jackson himself. And that was when she knew she loved him as a man, as a wolf and as everything he was. It was also when she realized she could never take him away from his family and his birthright.

"I don't think you'd fit into my world, Jackson." It took so much more courage than she'd imagined to turn down his offer. She knew she couldn't stay here with him, either. Not as a human.

"Could you, you know, do what Michael did to Lucy? If you bit me then I'd be like you."

"Stop!" Jackson turned on her with a horrified look on his face. "It's forbidden to change a human. Don't ever ask that of me again. And we have no guarantee that it wouldn't kill you, either. You may be willing to take that chance, but your life is much more precious to me in any form."

"How is it forbidden? I mean, I'm pretty new to all of this, but it seems to me that he did bite her."

"Michael was always the exception to the rules. I don't have those answers, Jessica."

"Then who does?"

•

Michael has answers, Jackson mused to himself, and at least one secret, too.

It was true his brother had broken all the rules, but he had done much more than that. He propagated with many females, turning some and casting off others without any apparent pattern. No shifter he had ever known, or even heard tell of, had been able to claim more than one mate. How did he do it?

"Please, Jessica." He urgently gripped her by the shoulders. "I know you've been through a lot and the last thing I want to do is leave you again. Don't give up on me, not now. I may be back with answers this time. And trust me when I say I won't stop trying until I find a way to make this right."

"I believe you." She looked up at him with her beautiful hazel eyes sparkling in the light.

Jackson couldn't get through the lodge fast enough. He'd intended to return to the old house where Michael kept Lucy anyway, but he certainly wasn't expecting to be invited by the man himself.

What could his brother possibly want? Whatever it was, it couldn't be as urgent as his own sudden need for answers. And that house—it felt so familiar to him, though he couldn't recall ever being there. Something about the smell of the place made him comfortable. Perhaps it was why Michael lingered there when he had never really established a home base for his renegade clan before.

He hadn't seen any sign of the outlaw pack when he'd been there, however. This was personal somehow. He would be cautious. Jackson never let his guard down when dealing with the Dark Breed, but he felt as if he had a certain amount of protection after the way Michael had treated Emily and Lucy. With any luck, it wasn't a simple ruse to make him feel safe enough to come alone.

He opened the door to the kitchen to find Meredith there. Her arms were crossed defensively over her silk blouse. She was as beautiful and flawless as ever, but her lips were pressed thin with worry. His mother was afraid, maybe for the first time he could ever remember. The scent of it rolled off her skin and she couldn't hide that.

"It's not safe for you to see Michael unaccompanied by some

type of protection. You don't know what kind of trap he could have waiting. It wouldn't be unheard of for him to behave in that manner. Where is this place he's found, anyway?"

"Spent all morning looking for it, did you mother?" He couldn't help the frustrated response and immediately felt bad for letting his control slip.

"I only want you to be safe." Her hand flew to her mouth as she smothered a sob. He couldn't doubt her sincerity because he had never seen her like this before. "I lost your father and then your brother after that. If anything happens to you it will be the end of me."

"Help me by telling me the truth." Jackson leaned forward and kissed her furrowed brow. He waited patiently for her to say something, anything. All she gave him was the anguish in her eyes. He understood through her tortured silence that his answers waited elsewhere.

He chose to travel by ATV. He wanted to keep his human form, somehow feeling closer to Jessica that way. He had to be careful with these new emotions he felt for the dark-haired beauty who waited for him back at the lodge. His strength, honor and pride allowed him to rule the family unconditionally. He had to find a way to temper the dominance of his role with the incredible love and desire she inspired within him.

Though he never would have thought it possible before, loving her made him a better man. One his father could be proud of, he hoped.

Jackson was so lost in thought he found himself on the grounds of the old estate before he realized it. He idled for a moment at the edge of the clearing and then cut the engine. The sound of birds and forest wildlife carried on all around him—a good sign. If some type of ambush awaited, the animals would be silent and he would sense tension in the air.

He decided to go forward on foot. The ATV would drown out all sound and scent until it was too late for him to pick up on the subtleties of the forest. Smoke curled up from the chimney and Jackson experienced the same unexpected feeling of home he had before.

He didn't bother to step gingerly on the porch. He remembered with uncanny accuracy which of the warped floorboards creaked and which ones didn't. It wasn't about that, now. Jackson wanted Michael to know he was there, but it was more than that. He longed to see his brother without using caution, without tiptoeing around and watching his back for danger.

Dammit, he missed him! He wanted to understand what Michael needed and longed to put his shattered family back together before they fell apart forever. If only his father was here to advise him, to help him through this seemingly insurmountable mountain of tasks.

He is here. I am his son and he will always be a part of me, Jackson reminded himself, opening the door. He crossed the foyer with strong, confident strides.

It was time to set things right, for everyone.

Chapter 16

"I only want to get Lucy's things. She'll rest easier if she has her handbag, believe me. It has everything she could want inside and I'll feel better when she feels better."

Jessica stood directly in front of Roland in the great hall. What she said was true enough. Lucy never went far without her bag of accessories so she knew he could see the honesty in her eyes. She just prayed he didn't think about how much easier it would be for him to retrieve those items himself.

"Jackson didn't tell you I couldn't come, did he?" she asked, doing her best to keep her tone reasonable. "I know how to run a four-wheeler, too. You don't have to piggy back with me."

"No, he didn't leave any instructions regarding your care and feeding in his absence." Roland frowned, probably wondering if her motives were genuine. "That doesn't mean he'd approve of it, however."

He's not convinced. I'm going to have to go for the Oscar here, she thought, changing tactics.

"You don't think it's still dangerous, do you?" Jessica feigned concern, taking a step closer to the young man. "I mean, I heard you tell Emily it was completely safe now. I guess you could've been trying to put on a brave face for her, after all. I wouldn't want her to know I was worried about going there, either."

"There's nothing to worry about, as I've said." His voice was dangerously low. Jessica's skin broke out in goosebumps. She had to remember she was dealing with a male who could revert to his primal emotions at any time. Though he wasn't leader of the clan, he was still strong and proud. Poking his ego with a stick probably wasn't the best idea, but she hadn't really been full of good ideas anyway as of late. She needed him to take her to the cabin. There was no way she could remember the trails back by herself and if Lucy's cell phone was still in the truck, no one else might have discovered it yet.

"I'm not a prisoner here, a hostage or something, am I?" This time the panic in her voice was real enough and Roland reacted to her immediately.

"Are you serious, Jessica? Don't you understand?" He grasped both of her hands and held them while he looked down into her eyes. "Everything Jackson does is to keep you safe. Do you really think he wants to hurt you? I've seen the way he looks at you, but even more importantly, I've seen the look in his eyes when you aren't even there."

His words struck a deep chord in her heart and she almost felt guilty for planning to contact the outside world. She didn't think Roland would understand, and she wasn't even sure she did herself. Somehow, if she could connect with reality for even a minute, then maybe she could accept that the other things around her were really happening too. Perhaps a call to Lucy's grandmother to let her know they were fine would do it. Knowing that she could phone out if she needed to would make all the difference in the world. She doubted the members of the Hart family would be inclined to agree, which was why she needed to do this on her own.

"Why don't you just tell me where the purse is and I'll grab it on the way back. If anything happened to you under my care, I'd never forgive myself." He meant it sincerely, she could see that, but she had to find a way for him to agree with her plan.

"Well, I guess that's all right." She allowed a pensive look to cross her face. "You'll have to make sure you get all three of the celebrity lipstick shades she just bought, the plum gloss, and the matching body lotion and perfume from her suitcase. They might be in the outside pocket, or inside beneath her underwear. She doesn't like for the bottles to break, you know, so she wraps them up in socks and things. I can make you a list, if you like. Do you have a notebook?"

Jessica almost burst out in laughter at the dazed look in his eyes.

"I'm sure if you stayed inside the station the entire time nothing could really happen to you, I'd think." She could see the wheels turning as he weighed his options.

"I'll let you decide, Roland. It doesn't really matter to me." She shrugged before she started to wander off. "Hey, is that the library over there? I've been meaning to pick up a new book."

"Jessica, wait," he called out to her before she'd gotten far. "I'll show you the library when we get back. Go grab your coat and meet me at the gate behind the courtyard. I'll go through the stable and bring the ATVs around back for us."

"You have a stable? Isn't that kind of … I don't know, strange to keep some animals in servitude considering your family's, uh, situation?"

"Back in the day we kept farm animals, I suppose. It's not like we could pop down to the local Walgreen's for a quart of milk and a loaf of bread a century ago, could we? At any rate, it's a garage now. Get your coat before I change my mind."

"I practically have it on." That much was true. Everytime she came downstairs she brought her coat with her and stashed it nearby. After what happened at the ranger station she wasn't eager to keep her cold weather gear too far from retrieval.

He disappeared down one of the side corridors in a flash. Jessica opened a nearby door to pull her thick coat off the topmost hinge. She was still zipping and buckling when she entered the kitchen and saw Jackson's mother slumped against the chair near the cast iron stove where Emily had been the evening before. The defeated posture didn't seem like her style and Jessica's observation proved correct as the elegant woman stiffened when she noticed her.

"Are you alright, Meredith?" Jessica was hesitant to approach the hostile woman in the corner.

"I don't know what you must think of me, young woman. Perhaps you view me as a monster, and maybe I am." Her words were so laden with sadness that Jessica felt a pang in her heart despite her caution.

"If you'd like the truth, I can honestly say I don't know what to think about anyone right now."

"I wanted to protect Emily at first, and then you came along with Lucy. Oh, how you reminded me of myself when I was young! I thought if I could save just one of you from my fate, from the pain."

Her voice dwindled off in anguish though Jessica was hanging on her every word. She waited a short time to see if Meredith would continue, but the woman had closed herself off again.

Jessica crossed the room despite her better judgment. She allowed her fingers to brush the woman's shoulder a moment, letting Meredith know she felt for her whether she wanted her empathy or not. As she was about to pull away, the older woman suddenly reached up and grabbed her hand, briefly laying her fingers against her porcelain cheek. Jessica could feel the hot tears against her skin and wondered what could be so heart wrenching that this proud woman could lose control.

A cold feeling gripped her stomach and settled there when she realized she was probably going to find out.

•

Jackson stood in the foyer of the battered farmhouse. A robust fire crackled in the sitting room to his left. He could see the wooden picture frame he'd carried upstairs was back in its place on the mantle.

This house meant something to Michael—all of it did. He was convinced now that his brother genuinely loved Lucy. Faint strains of music reached his ears—Mozart, Jackson thought he recognized the piece. The music came from the kitchen and Jackson proceeded with all his senses on alert through the swinging door to the other side. It was still daylight outside and the cold sun filtered through the tall windows above the sink and counters, bathing the area.

"You've got to be kidding me," he murmured to himself as he crossed the room to the cookstove in the corner. The white glaze was chipped in places, revealing black patches of steel underneath. This was a very old appliance, the kind that had to be lit with a match. And if dirty dishes were any evidence, the stove had been used recently.

His eyes trailed along the counter until they reached an open door. He caught the damp scent of the basement then, and again the smell of musty earth and dried spices from the cellar overwhelmed him with familiarity.

The music came from below, now that he had a point of reference, and Jackson could see flickers up the basement walls from whatever light source was down there.

Why would Michael be in the basement when he obviously took so much care with the rest of the house? There was only one way to find out, and he was tired of playing cat and mouse.

Jackson's heavy boot struck the first wooden step with an audible thud. It was his way of announcing his presence to Michael so his younger brother wouldn't be startled. He sensed no danger in being here, in this house, and for the first time in years he felt hope surrounding a meeting with his estranged sibling.

The firelight from a dozen candles lit the cellar room and brought to life the mural Michael was painting. Jackson's heart swelled when he caught sight of the peace in the colors before him. This illustration wasn't dark or lonely, not like the many Michael created before he left the family. This painting was full of light and beauty.

His brother gracefully guided the brush with a grand flourish and Jackson was beginning to wonder if he even knew he was standing there. It was an unspoken sign of trust that Michael allowed his back turned to him for such a long period of time. It didn't take long for him to verify they were completely alone—an olive branch Jackson didn't intend to turn down. With an easy gait he walked across the damp floor and stood directly next to his brother who hummed lightly as he stepped back to regard his work.

"Do you like it?" Michael asked. Hs voice was sweet again, tender and searching for his older brother's approval just as Jackson remembered it.

"I love it," Jackson answered with genuine emotion in his voice. It was an underwater landscape with a perfect image of Lucy rising from the sea like the Goddess Aphrodite. Her red hair cascaded over her shoulders and covered her alabaster skin in a natural drape of modesty. This stunning tribute was a work of art that the girl herself would never likely see.

"I'm so sorry, Michael. I know Reginald informed you of Lucy's condition and how dangerous it would be for you to contact her again."

"I don't believe there can be no other way, brother. Perhaps that's what you've been told all your life, much as I'd been. You can see for yourself that I exist outside the parameters that have been set up for our kind. How can I fail my love, now that my heart has made its choice?"

"How have you done it, Michael?" Jackson was suddenly urgent with the question. "We mate for life, and yet those rules don't seem to apply to you."

"You and I are so different, but in some respects we do follow the same path. I spent these last few years in search of what you so easily take for granted. I found I could have sex, but it never bonded me to any of the women. That place inside me remained cold and hollow. I became consumed with the need to find love. Like the absolute bond I could easily see between our parents, between all those in the family who had taken a mate."

"You could have come to me with this and I would have done anything to help you," Jackson said.

"How could I burden you, the next in line for the family rule? Many would cry favoritism when they'd discovered what I'd done. How many had I inadvertently turned or killed as I sought only love? By the time I realized what a mess I'd made it was far too late to do anything but leave. I thought I was broken, that I deserved to be an outcast. It wasn't until Lucy that I discovered the truth. The first moment I saw her face I felt what the bond really is. My fate was sealed in that instant, when I loved her."

"What irony that you found a woman at the end of your quest, one who must forever be human. As we well know, the two can't mix. I had hoped, perhaps ..." Jackson was distracted by his own thoughts, his own impossible feelings for Jessica. His brother's tragedy was right in front of him and he couldn't allow the same thing to happen to the woman he loved.

"It is truly ironic, but not for the reasons you may believe. It can be done, Jackson, and I have the proof right here."

Chapter 17

Jessica followed Roland as closely as she dared, not knowing the trails through the preserve very well. He was doing his best to maintain a safe, steady pace, though even that gave her much less time than she'd hoped to glance around for landmarks. Their tires left plenty of tracks out in the open fields and clearings they crossed, but when they were beneath the dense pines very little snow made it through the thick boughs to coat the forest floor.

She wouldn't be able to find her way from the lodge on her own. And if she could manage to escape, she'd be leaving her friends behind. As far as she could tell, the Hart clan themselves hadn't done anything to harm them. She couldn't even say they were kidnapped. Anyone she told would think she was crazy. Maybe they'd be right, too. Maybe she and Lucy were frozen half to death inside that rental truck on the side of the road and this was all just a hallucination. I have to try to get to that truck for sure, now.

Until she could get a handle on their situation and figure out what was reality, she was going to do whatever she could to keep some kind of control. And that meant getting her hands on Lucy's cell phone.

Roland slowed behind the cabin and idled ahead to the workshed where she knew they stored the ATVs. He cocked his head when they turned off the engines and she was sure he wasn't listening for the rangers—she'd heard enough to know something had happened to them. She shuddered at the thought of their time alone with Michael in the Hocking Hills estate. What might have happened to the two girls if Jackson's brother hadn't taken a shine to Lucy? She didn't think she'd be here to wonder about it, that much was certain.

"Hand them over." Roland's voice cut through her macabre

reverie and she realized he was pointing to the pocket of her jeans where she had slipped the ignition key for the ATV.

At first she thought to take umbrage over his insinuation she might run away. She couldn't be mad though, of course she had considered it. But with the way sound carried through the woods she knew she probably couldn't even get the engine cranked before Roland caught her at it.

"Fine, you can have them. If something comes chasing us out of the house, though, you better make sure my four-wheeler is ready first!"

"We're fine. There's nothing in the area aside from a few chipmunks and a bunny or two. Don't be so nervous."

They walked to the front porch together. "Just get what you came for," Roland instructed her firmly. "I'll measure the bedroom window and head to the workshop to cut the plywood. If you come out and don't see me, I'll be behind the shed cleaning a few things out so just wait for me inside the cabin."

He's looking for the rangers too, I'll bet, Jessica thought. He doesn't want me to see anything he might have to dispose of. By now someone must be missing them. He'd probably report it to the local authorities himself and if they found anything, there'd be no doubt it was an animal attack.

"It'll take me a minute to pick up her things. If you want, I can make sure the coals are out in the fireplace and no power is left on or food rotting in the sink."

"Thank you, Jessica," Roland said as he looked her over with newly appraising eyes. "I'm sorry I didn't trust you at first. You have to understand we're all feeling our way here."

Did she really blame them? It wasn't like they could go around announcing their furry family lineage to everyone they met. Jackson made it clear he hid the truth to protect her. Even Emily insisted that without Roland's intervention she'd be dead from the attack she suffered during her mountain hike.

Well, she'd try not to hold anything against them as long as they did the same with her. If Roland caught her today, however, she didn't think he'd be so forgiving. He finished with the measuring tape and nodded to her briefly before exiting the door through the kitchen.

Jessica spent a few minutes looking busy around the counter

tops, running water in the blackened pot of charcoal beef stew in case it could possibly help. She didn't get the feeling that Roland was spying on her actions. She heard the droning sound of a saw coming from the workshop. It was now or never, so Jessica slipped out of the kitchen and through the front door.

She stood on the porch for a moment and searched the woods around the cabin for any sign of danger. The winter sun was high in the sky, but the feeble light it cast didn't do much to warm her as she set off down the path through the trees.

She walked for a short while until she couldn't hear Roland's saw any longer. For some reason the hike seemed a lot farther now than it had the night they abandoned the truck. Every step she took toward the isolated road increased her apprehension. Every branch that creaked and twig that snapped set her on edge until she realized her shoulders were tight with tension.

Jessica looked at her watch when she came to the edge of the forest. Snow drifted across the open plain and froze on the surface in waves. There was no sign at all of the footsteps that led them there, and she squinted against the pale light in the distance. She could see the truck right where they left it! The four wheel drive remained lopsided in the ditch, snow covering most of the silver paint.

Maybe her luck was changing after all. Jessica picked up the pace, a little less cautious now that she was through the trees and her goal was in sight. She slowed when she neared the rental, trying Roland's listening trick. Unfortunately, all she could hear was the wind whistling through the creaking branches of the pines. The hair stood up on the back of her neck in warning, but she couldn't see anything around her that might pose a threat. Still, she hunched down into the snow on the road, attempting to peer beneath the truck in case something might be lurking there.

The snow had drifted underneath the chassis, but it was pristine and undisturbed. Jessica walked up to the passenger side and wiped her gloved hand across the window. A thick layer of ice had frozen onto the glass, making it impossible for her to see inside without a scraper.

She looked one more time over her shoulder at the empty field behind her and felt safe enough to try the handle. The door was frozen shut. She pulled a number of different ways, with her boot propped up on the runner for leverage.

Damn, she was going to have to try the driver's door. The snow was deeper on that side and she had the ditch to navigate, but at least the wind was coming from the other direction. Jessica jumped the area where she calculated the burrow to be deepest and sunk past her knees in the icy drift. She grasped the handle and pulled with all her strength. The door swung open and she landed on her backside in the snow.

Lucy's red cell phone sat in plain view on the passenger side seat, still plugged into the charger.

Please, oh please, have a little bit of power left, Jessica fervently thought to herself as she crawled forward to grab the bottom of the door. As if reading her thoughts the mobile beeped ominously, indicating a low battery. Of course, Lucy got fifty voice mails a day. Whatever charge the thing might have built up would be drained by a message alert every handful of minutes.

She pulled herself across the driver's seat and laid her hands on the cold rubber of the phone case, unplugging the cable as quickly as possible. Four full bars of service showed in the left hand corner, but the battery icon flashed near empty.

She was about to climb the rest of the way inside to get out of the frosty air when a heavy thud struck the passenger side of the truck, shifting it dangerously. Her first instinct was to jump out of the vehicle and into the ditch, but she quickly discovered she couldn't stay there long as the chill from the bitterly cold snow seeped into her bones.

The sound of someone trying to open the frozen door reached her ears and she didn't think a wolf would be able to grapple with the handle.

"Please, open!" Jessica was shocked to hear the panic filled voice from the other side and slowly crawled around the front of the grill to get a better look.

A man with no coat on pulled at the door in frustration. His clothing was torn and bloody, but Jessica could see it was some type of uniform. He wouldn't last long in the elements without cold weather gear so she pushed forward, pulling off her down-filled parka at the same time.

"Here, put this on." She hurried to the man but he hadn't seen her coming. He fell to the side, crawling backward in fear before he realized she wasn't a threat.

"Oh, thank God!" he exclaimed, trying to stand. She was already frozen half to death without her coat and she was wearing several layers. The injured man must be close to frostbite by now. She noticed an insignia on his tan colored shirt and thought she saw the word "preserve" stitched near a number. There was so much blood on his uniform she couldn't tell how hurt he was, but her first priority was to get him wrapped up.

"Do you have a cell phone with you? Please, help us!" His knees sagged a little when she got her coat over his broad shoulders and she leaned him against the side of the truck.

"Is the other ranger nearby?" She asked urgently, dialing 911 without any thought of the consequences for the Hart family. He said "us" so she assumed there was one more person in need of help.

Jessica read the number right off his shirt to the answering operator. She hoped it gave them their location or at least an idea of the vicinity. When she was calmly asked what the nature of the emergency was, she said animal attack. They wanted to know what type of animal and Jessica hesitated then. What if she said wolf and they came hunting them? What if they caught Roland, or even Emily?

In the end it didn't matter because the battery on Lucy's phone died before she could answer.

That was when she saw the speck in the distance. It moved toward them without a doubt and at an alarming pace. At first she assumed it was Roland and though she knew he would be terribly angry with her, he'd be grateful she'd found one of the rangers.

As the solitary runner grew closer Jessica saw it was a wolf that she had not seen before. This animal was nearly all white with a touch of pale grey fur around its neck. Without thinking she stepped in front of the semi-conscious man as the wolf closed the final distance between them. Jessica braced herself for impact but the wolf slowed to a stop. The animal seemed intelligent, looking at her with crystal blue eyes.

When she relaxed her muscles, the white wolf growled low but turned in the opposite direction. Her attention was drawn to the tree line again and she saw the two figures tracking prints in the snow. They were human, but something about their manner gave her an ominous feeling.

The wolf crouched low on the road as the man and woman grew closer, and she could see the hackles rising on the back of its neck. Her whole body was one giant shiver of uneasiness and she understood why as the source approached.

The man was massive in height and held a crossbow over his arms, fully loaded and ready. His broad shoulders were draped in what looked like newly skinned wolf pelts. She tried to tell herself it was some other kind of animal but there was no mistaking the fur. Jessica's hand flew to her mouth, partially to cover the sob in her throat that reacted to the mantle the man wore, but also to repress the retching reflex in the pit of her stomach. This must be someone from the renegade pack she'd heard about.

What if one of those hides was Roland, or worse … Jackson?

"Did you think you could keep him all for yourself, Anna Lisa?" The lead male spoke directly to the wild animal that remained crouched low to the ground between them. She was about to spring; Jessica could see the twitching muscles in her hind legs. She couldn't let the wolf sacrifice herself to protect them when help was coming.

"I really don't think Michael would approve this type of treatment for the rangers, do you?" Jessica boldly addressed the dominant male and his female counterpart sneered in derision, flipping her finely woven black braids over her shoulder.

"Michael is weak, not worthy to lead the Dark Breed pack." He almost spat the words as he said them. "Do you know he wanted to rejoin his little family in the hills? He thought we'd be content under Jackson's thumb, relegated to being the black sheep born on the dark spot of the Hart bloodline."

"Surely not everyone thinks that way in your tribe." Jessica was stalling for time now. She really didn't imagine she could get anywhere with the conversation, but every minute she kept him talking was a minute longer the authorities had to rescue them.

"And surely, as you say, not all of them did." The man laughed and stroked the furs on his shoulder to illustrate his point. "Anna Lisa will be the next to join my heritage cloak. She thought she'd protect our troublesome ranger friend here, bring him back to Jackson maybe and be welcomed into the family with open arms. Who knows?"

"Who cares?" his black-haired companion said. "Michael had his chance to bond me, and yet he chose some fragile human as his bride. I found another fine specimen to step up, did I not, Justin?"

"And that is what I intend to do, Bria my love." The male leveled the crossbow at the white wolf who refused to back down and leave them exposed.

"Don't hurt her!" The ranger suddenly cried, falling between the animal and the arrow's line of sight a split second before the trigger was pulled.

The bolt from the bow hit him square in the shoulder, throwing him over the wolf and against the vehicle at their backs. Jessica was astonished by how powerful such a primitive weapon could be.

"That's touching." Justin's tone said otherwise as he clicked another bolt in place and aimed at the wolf. Before he could let it fly, the sound of a siren blared in the distance. The red flashing lights of an emergency vehicle reflected off the frozen snow.

"Damn," the dark woman whispered under her breath and pulled on her consort's arm. "There will be time for this later. Now we must flee."

The couple sprinted side by side toward the forest, but the wolf remained with her injured companion. The ranger looked bad enough to her before he got shot; now Jessica didn't know if he had any hope of survival.

"You have to leave now," she whispered to their protector. "I promise I'll keep him safe."

The wolf faced her and looked her in the eye. Jessica was shaken by the clarity of its action. She felt in her heart that she understood the animal on the most primitive of levels.

The emergency vehicle struggled through to their location and only then did the white wolf run. An older gentleman dressed as a sheriff pulled himself out of the truck and put his hand on his side arm when he reached the wounded ranger. His eyes watched the wolf as she faded into the distance.

"Please, don't hurt her!" Jessica managed to choke out, terrified the old man would fire on the creature that had saved them.

"No, not her," he stated simply, and she realized his watery grey eyes were scanning the horizon for anything that might stop the wolf's retreat.

Chapter 18

"What proof can you possibly have, Michael?"

Jackson began to pace nervously. Though he couldn't believe what his brother was saying, his pulse leapt at the possibility there could still be a way for him to be with Jessica. He forced himself to realize he couldn't allow false hope to taint his judgment, and quashed the sentiment at once. He didn't think he could live with himself if he ever caused her harm.

"Just look at these." Michael pulled a heavy box from one of the darkened corners of the cellar and gingerly lifted out one of many books.

Jackson opened the cover. The pages were written with an elegant and precise hand. The paper was yellow and crisp, and it was difficult to read the faded ink by candle light.

"What are they? Where did you get them?"

"I found them here in the attic. They're our mother's journals."

"Why would something like this be hidden in a decrepit old farmhouse that has been empty for years?" Jackson couldn't accept the validity of the discovery. He had always thought his mother to be strong and private, not the type to chronicle her feelings on paper.

"These books are here because this is where she lived. This is where our father brought her and where they stayed together in secret before he turned her. She was a normal girl, the same as Lucy—and Jessica." Michael carefully studied his face to see his reaction to the outrageous claim, but Jackson could barely register the implications.

"That can't be true. You don't know what you're saying!"

There were reasons it was built into their code, the law against mating with humans. It almost always killed them. It was best to stay with their own kind. And the patriarch of the clan, their father, would never do such a thing regardless. His bride would have to be of the breed to keep the bloodline pure.

"The only truth I know is what I have read inside these pages, brother." Michael set the remaining books at his feet.

"You can take them if you want. Did you not wonder why this house felt so familiar when you first came? You were born here, but that's not the secret our mother hides. Father knew when he courted her that he could never turn her, but he hopelessly loved her from the very first day he came across her in the Hocking Hills. He was there to oversee the construction on the estate house at the preserve and found he was unable to part with her, despite her humanity."

"She came with him willingly? She felt the same for him?"

"Oh, Jackson." Michael smiled brilliantly. "She loved him more than anything in the world and her journals are filled with stunning prose of longing and passion. I never would have imagined such a thing from her."

"Tell me what you know of her secret and why she can't share it with me."

"We have always been told that it's not possible, but while they lived here together she became pregnant—with you. They both knew you would never be accepted by the family under the circumstances and so they chose to risk her life and yours by attempting to turn her with you in her womb."

"If anyone ever found about this, if they discovered my true blood lineage—" Jackson couldn't finish the sentence. His father did what he had to do in order to protect his love and his first-born son. No wonder it was a secret she felt she must take to the grave.

"Why do you show this to me now? What do you have to gain?"

"I wanted you to understand our parents so you can understand me." Michael cast a glance back to the wall where his goddess rose eternally from the sea. "I need your help. Father was working on a formula that could make me human. It's the only way I'll ever be able to love Lucy without endangering her."

"He died testing that formula! I can't allow you to take that risk."

"And I can't go on without knowing I pursued all avenues to be with her. Ask mother about the formula. She knows more about it than she admits. Her words hint at the fact in her journals and now she will have to tell you the truth."

"Impossible. The formula was not created until years after you were born."

"So she said to you. The proof is at your feet, Jackson. Will you help me?"

"Your motive in all of this is love?"

"I don't know how else to prove that is the case, except to remind you that I let Lucy go back with you. I knew she would be safe at the Hart House until I could regain control of my followers."

Jackson considered the meaning of Michael's admission. How all this time he was worried he was losing control over his family because the Dark Breed was so strong. They must not have approved his brother's choices any more than his mother approved of Jessica, and fractured because of it.

But if Michael had lost what tenuous hold he was able to exert over his little flock then they were all in serious danger. He needed to get back to the compound immediately and warn the family. And this time he would get the answers he needed from his mother.

"Come with me, Michael. I promise no harm will befall you at the lodge as long as we are together."

"There are still those who follow me and are good at heart. If I join you now I doubt they'll have a chance of survival. Just find out about the formula, Jackson. I think it could be the key to resolving everything."

"I'll be back for the rest of the books, Michael." Jackson promised his brother solemnly as he tucked the first journal inside his jacket. "And I'll come back for you. We will work this out, together."

Jackson traversed the trails back to the lodge like a madman. What did his mother know about the formula that she wasn't telling him? Michael was right about one thing—she would finally be forced to reveal the truth to him. He would allow for nothing less.

Now he understood how far his brother's control over the renegade pack had slipped. Instead of feeling fear at the danger, he became enveloped by an all-encompassing need to protect his family and the woman he loved.

For the first time since he was given the reins as the head of the

Hart dynasty he was sure about his position and capabilities.

Jackson knew then that he could have it all. It was true—where there was love there would always be a way. His father had proven just that and he vowed to do the same with Jessica. Now that he no longer had to repress his feelings for her he felt a strength flowing through his veins that he never realized he could possess.

He hit the brakes so hard the ATV skidded up to the front of the lodge. He was off the vehicle before the motor cut out. He took the roughly hewn stone steps three at a time, barreling through the front door.

Meredith was standing in the open foyer, a look of worry on her face. She opened her mouth to speak just as her eyes fell on the journal he clutched tightly to his chest.

"Oh, God," she whispered, covering her lips with shaky fingers. She swayed slightly on her feet and Jackson sprung forward in alarm to catch her. She weighed almost nothing in his arms as he half-held, half-carried her into the library.

"I am sorry, so sorry," Meredith repeated several times, her face buried in her hands to muffle her cries.

"I wanted to tell you, but I made a promise to your father. Even after he passed I couldn't bring myself to break faith with him. Your birth was the last secret we shared and I couldn't let go of the one thing we had together that was sacred."

Jackson watched his mother with awe. He had never seen her cry before a day in his life. He couldn't be angry with her in any way for hiding the secret and honoring her word to his father. There still remained the matter of Jessica, however.

"Even knowing the truth, you still attempted to separate me from Jessica in order to protect me. How could you look me in the eye every day and deceive us?"

She raised her head then and regarded him with confusion.

"Do you really think I was protecting you? I was protecting her! No one but our kind can know the absolute pain of losing their mate. I was trying to save her from the same fate that befell me. Every morning when I wake, my heart screams for the loss of the only man I will ever love and I pray that will be the day I die!"

So this is what it means to give your soul completely to the bond.

"I promise you, Mother. I will not turn her. But if she'll have me

I'll never let her go, and I certainly won't apologize to anyone for my love."

"I know you mean what you say." She sighed and gave him a look of sympathy. "I was also given the choice. Remember that Jessica has a will and a heart of her own."

"Your journals talk about the formula. I understood it wasn't developed until Michael split away from the family, but he tells me now that is not the case."

"Michael has changed so much in the past few years." She looked almost wistful when she spoke his name. "I've been talking with Lucy as she recovers. I used to carry so much guilt over his nature, you realize. I considered he was so unusual because my blood muddied the waters perhaps. I had you, though, my strong and handsome first-born. Now I see that love has made the difference in both my children."

"It has made a world of difference for me. But tell me about the formula, Mother. Please. We're running out of time."

"The truth is so painful to relate. Your father first developed it for the love of me. He thought he could become human because it was forbidden to turn me. I never wanted him to change for me. I couldn't permit such a thing."

"But you allowed him to take it for Michael's sake?" Jackson had a hard time keeping his voice down and he looked around, remembering where they were.

"I never allowed him to do anything! He took the damn potion on his own and left me with one son who wasn't ready and a deviant child he died for. Later, long after the failure, the doctor told me it was developed from my own blood. He thought it may have failed because it might only work on those born from me or turned by my children."

The bitterness in her voice was terrible and he knew the secret must have been a heavy burden for her all these years. Even indirectly, she contributed to the cause of his death.

All of that was different now. He was ready, finally, and he would take his rightful place at the head of the family without shame. And he'd do it with his woman at his side.

"Is Jessica in her room? I need to speak with her right away."

"Actually, that's why I was standing in the foyer when you arrived. She's missing. She and Roland never came back from the ranger station this morning."

Chapter 19

"You're taking us back to the lodge? This man needs a hospital right away."

Jessica's voice was strained as she glanced back at the wounded ranger in the rear seat of the sheriff's truck. Her heart wanted to return to the house more than anything and tell Jackson the truth, but what would he think after he discovered what she'd done? One call to 911 put everyone under a microscope and she hadn't considered the repercussions for one moment.

"Listen to me carefully, young lady. You have no idea how lucky you were that I was close by when your call came in." The seasoned officer kept his eyes on the trail as he carefully navigated the pitfalls, but his tone held her attention completely. "I know it may be difficult for you to understand right now, but the best care this man could receive is at the medical facilities inside the Hart compound. He would never make it to a hospital, even if we called life flight. And when he arrived they wouldn't realize how to help him if he did survive the trip."

"You know about them, don't you?"

"I know enough."

Whatever his situation was with the Hart family, he wasn't going to blow the whistle. She hoped Roland was safe at the cabin. Those two crazy people had gone in that direction. She wanted to ask the officer if they could stop but another look at the injured man in the back seat gave her the obvious answer. It was slow going in the larger vehicle. The sheriff was forced to keep to more open trails and old access roads that ran along fields from back in the day when farmers had lived on the land. She dreaded this journey because it gave her time to think about all the ways Jackson could be angry with her tonight.

It was nearly dark by the time they reached the lodge. Every light at the Hart House was blazing through the windows. They must all be on high alert by now. She hoped it wasn't a sign that something far worse had happened. They were met at the front of the manor by several members of the family before the truck rolled to a stop. There was a lot of shouting once they discovered the ranger in the back. Jessica noted with interest that they treated the sheriff with deference and respect.

She, on the other hand, was almost completely ignored as she wandered around aimlessly on the flagstones of the front landing. Her coat was still on the injured man, but she didn't feel the cold anymore. She knew once she was inside she'd have to face Jackson and the thought chilled her more than the night air.

"Jessica?" a voice exclaimed in surprise from the doorway leading into the manor. Emily emerged, slipping gracefully through the throng that milled chaotically on the steps. "What in the world are you doing out here? It's not safe. Roland went straight to Jackson and Sheriff Winters was right behind him. There's going to be some kind of important family meeting. The last thing we need is Jackson worrying over where you are."

"So Roland is fine?"

"I'm not going to lie to you, my dear friend. I think he's mad at you. He said you ran off at the ranger station and by the time he tracked you down you were already under the supervision of the sheriff."

"Emily, I should have told you what I was doing. Maybe even mentioned it to Roland, I don't know." She allowed herself to be led into the foyer.

People stood together in groups all around them, talking in hushed tones. Dozens of eyes glanced toward the study and back frequently.

"What were you thinking anyway? Jackson was ready to have Roland's head when he found out what happened."

She was about to answer Emily when she realized the thick cluster of people around them had quieted; they were probably quite interested in what she had to say.

"Can we go upstairs? I really need to get out of these wet clothes." It was a perfectly good excuse to leave. Her jeans were heavy and soaked from her trudge through the snow and now that she was inside, the feel of them against her skin was almost unbearable. Once they were out of earshot she felt more comfortable confiding in Emily.

"Okay, I went to collect some of Lucy's things, which I'm sure Roland mentioned, but I also wanted to see about getting Lucy's cell phone."

"Are you crazy? Why would you walk all the way to the edge of the property line to get a phone?" Emily actually paused in the hallway outside Jessica's door, a look of disbelief on her face.

"I wanted to make sure we had a way of reaching the outside world. You have to admit all of this must seem out of control to me! I want us to be safe, Emily. I won't apologize for trying to have a plan in place for the three of us. Has it occurred to you that Lucy's grandmother must be worried half to death by now?"

"Well, she's not." Emily walked past Jessica and into her guest suite. "Now come inside."

"How do you know that?"

"Because Jackson gave us the satellite phone earlier so Lucy and I could call her. What do you think is going on here? Has anyone in the Hart family done anything at all to make you think you were a prisoner? I love that you want to protect us. That's a part of who you are, Jessica, and probably the reason we all survived our childhood! It's probably also the reason that you can't see all the things Jackson is doing to protect you right now. If you'd like to leave it will be no problem, I can arrange for it. But know that Lucy and I have chosen to stay."

Jessica felt ridiculous. Emily was right on all counts. It would take a strong woman to be a part of Jackson's life, but she would have to learn to place her fate in the hands of the man she loved. He must also be able to trust her as much as she would him.

"I'd like to stay for now, too, Emily. Thank you for talking to me."

"That's what friends are for, right? Now why don't you have a hot bath and relax? I have a feeling it's going to be a long night."

Jessica didn't think she'd be able to take Emily's advice, but once she lowered her aching limbs into the steaming, lavender-scented water her whole body let go. It felt wonderful to shed all the tension she'd carried on her shoulders since this crazy adventure began.

Her friend had taken all her wet clothing and left behind some things for her to wear. As far as Jessica knew her suitcase was still back in the rental truck and she certainly wasn't going to ask anyone if she could go get it.

The fragrant bath was so heavenly that she submerged her entire body and ran her fingers through her hair under the water. She didn't expect to see Jackson this evening, not with all the turmoil happening within the family.

She reluctantly left the bath, but only after the water cooled enough to drive her out. Her skin was soft and supple beneath the heavy cotton towel and she could see a lustrous sheen on her dark hair in the nearby mirror. Her steps made no sound on the plush carpet as she crossed into the bedroom to rifle through the clothes Emily had stacked neatly on the king-sized bed.

Her friend always wore the latest fashions and was the most stylish of the bunch, so she didn't know why she expected anything less from the loaned clothing. After a quick inspection she discovered the only sleepwear Emily had afforded her was an emerald silk gown. The fabric was luxurious as she slipped it over her head, but though it fell to her toes she felt exposed beneath the thin spaghetti straps and figure hugging cut. Fortunately the gown came with a matching robe, which she put on immediately.

A large mirror sat above the vanity table on the other side of the room and as she walked toward it she could barely believe it was her own image in the reflection. Her hair was almost black when it was wet, and it cascaded over her shoulders in a wave of glossy curls that she had never been able to tame. The color of the gown brought out the depths of her hazel eyes and the soft shades of golden makeup Emily left on the table highlighted their sparkle.

Just sitting in that sumptuously appointed room, all pampered and perfumed, felt surreal. All her life she'd done her duty, taken care of everyone and everything around her. Ever since she arrived at Hart House Jackson had been taking care of her, no matter how she tried to thwart his tender plans. And it felt good!

The knock on the door startled her because she hadn't expected Emily to be back so soon. For a moment her stomach dropped nervously when it occurred to her it could be Jackson. All her alone time hadn't prepared her for seeing him again as well as she'd thought.

"Come in," she called from her place at the vanity.

The door opened silently and though it wasn't Jackson, she wasn't a bit relieved. Meredith entered the room, her eyes sweeping over Jessica's sitting figure. She stood at once, not knowing what treatment to expect or the things Jackson's mother could possibly have to say to her.

"Won't you join me on the couch?" Meredith gestured formally to the same spot she and Emily had just occupied a short time ago.

Jessica walked toward the visitor. Her arms clutched the folds of her robe, holding it shut though she had knotted the belt twice. She perched on the edge of the settee, her back stiff and uncomfortable as Meredith sat next to her.

"I won't insult your intelligence with small talk, young lady. It's clear to me that would be unworthy of your time. If you'll allow me, I have something important to say and I'd like you to consider my words carefully."

"Please, go ahead." Jessica appreciated her frankness. Despite her strained encounters with the woman in the past, she had come to respect certain aspects of her personality.

"I have reason to believe you will soon be presented with a choice. I came here to tell you my last secret, one that Jackson's father and I have never spoken of to anyone. I think you should know what your options are when that time comes."

Jessica's eyes grew wide as Meredith leaned forward and whispered in her ear.

Chapter 20

The doctor had been very reluctant to give the formula over to Jackson. He assured the physician he had no intention of allowing Michael the use of it, and that was true. He would rather die himself than condemn his brother to an uncertain death. There was no way to prove the formula would be successful on any child born to Meredith unless he tested it himself.

You could be with Jessica if you succeeded—give her a normal life. The thought crept in to his mind even as he tried to prevent it.

Now that he was alone, he had time to consider future possibilities. The family was in crisis right now, but it was also closer than it had been in years to being whole again. He was the only person who could bring resolution to the situation Michael had placed on their doorstep. Jackson reached across the surface of his marble desk and grasped the plain package that contained the vials of serum. It wasn't necessary for him to hold the dangerous formula, yet he had insisted the doctor relinquish it. He was playing with an idea so close to his heart he didn't dare admit it to himself.

It was time for him to see Jessica. Any hopes regarding his future would be foolish if he didn't know where she ultimately stood. Unwilling to leave the box unguarded, he picked it up as he left the study. Many members of the family remained outside his door and they perked up when he exited, closing the panel behind him securely. He nodded to those nearest, but had no intention of stopping.

The hour was so late, what if she was sleeping? He wouldn't blame her if she'd arranged to leave the manor house by now, as often as he'd abandoned her to attend business. But everything he did regarding his family was ultimately to protect her. He felt selfish but he couldn't wait another day, not even another minute, to discover if she loved him as he loved her.

Their future would come to a crossroads tonight, one that would alter the lives of everyone he knew. His heart raced at the thought of everything that could change, and for the things he hoped would.

Jackson stood outside the guest suite door, drawing a deep breath. So much depended on the woman inside. She could be his forever if she desired it. Now he knew why he had never fallen in love, why he never took a mate out of obligation to please the family. There was only one woman in the world that roused him, drove him to distraction and brought out a passion inside him he never believed could exist. He needed to be with her, but he would give her the choice and accept her decision no matter what.

Jackson raised his hand to knock, telling himself if she didn't respond he shouldn't wake her. As his knuckles brushed against it, the door swung inward a few inches.

His heart sunk in a moment of icy fear. Why was the door not only unlocked, but ajar as well? With the family on guard tonight it would be difficult for a renegade member of the Dark Breed to creep into the manner, but after Michael's easy entry the other evening he knew it was possible.

It was very dark inside and he paused to listen carefully. The sounds of a fire crackled across the room but he wasn't able to pick up any other noise that would indicate distress. In fact, he couldn't hear anything else at all. Was she even inside?

"Jessica? I'm coming in." His voice was firm as he announced himself, weighing the aspect of surprise against propriety.

It took a moment for his eyes to adjust to the gloom, but when he saw her standing next to the fireplace he lost his breath. She was wearing an exquisite gown that draped over her pale shoulders, falling gently over her full breasts and hips. Her silken hair had dried in waves of curls down her back and she twisted a strand nervously between her graceful fingers.

Say something, say anything, you fool! The silent words echoed through his mind but he was so filled with the sudden desire for her that he was afraid to use his voice. She shifted slightly, and the silk fabric that caressed her shimmered in the firelight.

Jackson was held helpless in the doorway. It was as if every fiber in his being was acutely sensitive to the woman across the room. The pleasurable wave that encompassed him was almost painful as his desire for her became indescribable.

You need to leave here. You don't have control of yourself! His mind was rational enough to insert the plea, but his heart hammered so violently that it drowned out caution.

Jessica took a step forward, clearly confused by his inaction. Being that much closer set him over the edge. His shaking fingers set the box of vials down on the floor near the door frame. He had to pull himself together. What must she think of him?

•

Oh, Jackson was so mad at her.

Jessica knew he would come to her room sooner or later to read her the riot act. After what she'd done she could hardly blame him, either. But waiting for it to happen set her on edge. She had opened the guestroom door so many times to look down the hall she eventually left it open a crack in case she had a chance to hear anything that might be going on.

And now he stood with his muscular frame blocking out the light of the corridor and shaking with anger. Well, she would take whatever he had to give because she was the kind of woman who owned up to her actions. There wasn't any way for her to go back and change the things that happened, but she was more than willing to make it up to him in the future—if he gave her the chance.

He hadn't moved for so long, she realized he was waiting for her to invite him inside. Another faux pas on her part, Jessica imagined he must think her so rude! "I didn't expect to see you tonight," she hastily explained, crossing over to the sofa and retrieving her robe, which she slipped over her nightgown before belting it closed. "I'm glad you came. Would you like to sit?"

Jackson nodded in response and she was a bit unnerved he hadn't actually spoken yet. He crossed the room on what looked like auto pilot and sat woodenly on the couch. She stood nearby but didn't join him.

"I am so sorry, Jackson." The words left her mouth and though she had practiced her speech all through the night, it came out in a devastated tone. She hadn't meant for so much feeling to enter into it. "I have no right to be a guest in your house when I've caused your family nothing but trouble. I know that. My father always said it took a big man to apologize for his mistakes, but my mother said it took a better woman to do the same. I am not asking for clemency I don't deserve and if you can't forgive me then I will leave right away."

"Jessica, please." His voice was ragged, distraught, and she looked at his extended hand in confusion. Did he want her to shake goodbye with him? If that was the case, it was the least she could do in order to part with him in a civil manner.

She placed her delicate fingers inside his large, upturned palm. She expected a polite grip, but he closed his fingers over her firmly. His thumb rubbed the back of her knuckles and when she looked into his eyes to fathom what he was thinking she was surprised by what she saw there.

"Come here," he whispered, pulling her closer to him. Jessica was perplexed by the look on his face and when the back of her legs brushed up against his knees she found herself sitting on his lap.

He buried his face against her neck, pulling her hand up to his cheek and placing it there. He held her against his rough jaw even as she held him. His breath fell rapidly against her chest and she realized the silk night gown left very little between her skin and his attention.

"I love you, Jessica." As he spoke his lips brushed her neck, sending shivers through out her body. "From this moment forward I will love you every single day for the rest of my life; even if you choose to leave me that will never change. You will always have my heart."

"What can I expect if I stay?" she asked breathlessly, wondering a little if she was dreaming.

Jackson ran his strong fingers along her spine while his other arm encircled her. She was pressed firmly onto his lap and she could feel him pulse against the back of her thighs. The longing inside her was so profound she didn't think she could survive if Jackson wasn't willing to make love to her this time.

"If you stay I will give you everything."

She didn't have to ask what everything was. Her heart and her soul knew from the very first moment she laid eyes on him. She was so amazed that this magnificent man had chosen her that she couldn't respond.

His right hand slid the strap of her nightgown over her shoulder, exposing her skin to his mouth. He ran his lips along her collar bone, the feel of his breath hardening her nipples in anticipation. His fingers stroked the small of her back and she arched against his mouth, her body begging for him to give her the kisses she longed for.

His tongue found her aching nipple, licking it gently at first to judge her reaction. She squirmed wildly on his lap in response, moaning as he took her fully into his mouth. Her free hand pulled the shirt off his right shoulder and she grasped his neck with passionate strength as she held onto his body.

Jessica was nearly at her breaking point and swiveled on his lap to straddle his hips. Her borrowed gown slid up her thighs and she pressed herself firmly against him. He sharply drew a breath at the feel of her molded so perfectly to him, even through his clothing. She opened his pants out of pure need, releasing him from his restrictive clothing.

He was heavy in her hand as she pulled him free. It was her turn to gasp as she ran her palm over the hard length of him. He was as well endowed there as he was in all other aspects of his physical nature. Jessica held him in her right hand and wrapped herself around the base of his erection.

Her desire for him ran so deep that she slid herself against him, almost blind with the pleasure it gave her. Jackson's moan was the most passionate sound she'd ever heard. He grasped her hips with his huge hands and just as she thought he would push himself inside her, he held her still.

"Oh please, Jackson. Don't stop this time."

"Jessica, you must say to me that this is your choice. If we do this you can never leave me. We will always be together no matter the consequences."

She stopped her movements and looked him in the eye. He was completely serious in every way. And so was she.

"Jackson, take me to bed."

He picked her up like she was nothing, but wasn't rushed or primal like he had been at the beginning. He put her down on the satin comforter with a gentle touch and ran his hands over her body until she thought she couldn't stand any more foreplay.

"Don't make me wait." She strained to press her body against his.

"I want to remember this night for the rest of my life," he whispered in her ear, causing her to shiver. She grabbed his wandering hand and slid it between her legs, wanting him to touch her there. His fingers were strong as he pleasured her in ways she had no idea could be done.

"Do it or stop!" She finally raised her voice in frustration, her entire body a quivering mass.

"You didn't say the right words." Jackson propped himself on one elbow, releasing her from his touch.

This was her moment of choice. She thought of the advice she'd been given, of the secrets that must be kept. The decision was monumental.

"I love you."

Jackson released a breath she hadn't realized he'd been holding. He knelt between her legs, his hands stroking her outer thighs as he bent down to kiss her. He was so tender now, so attentive to her every response.

He tried to be gentle as he entered her. Jessica wrapped herself around him as best she could, but his enormous nature dictated they go slowly. Every single inch that pushed inside her filled her with insurmountable pleasure and as her cries of ecstasy grew Jackson was further emboldened to plunge deeper, satisfying his own needs.

Jessica found herself at the threshold of heaven. She knew Jackson was close and so she was aware that the true choice she had been given was upon her.

Her lover gasped and thrust himself deeply inside just as the height of orgasm engulfed her with mind-bending pleasure.

It was now or never.

Jessica held her partner tightly against her as he rode the waves of their height together. When Jackson reached his peak of fulfillment she chose her destiny so that he would not be forced to do it for them.

She bit him.

Chapter 21

Jackson was in the throes of unimaginable ecstasy when he felt Jessica reach her peak and clench passionately around him. Her release skyrocketed his climax past the boundaries of reason. Jackson lost all awareness of his surroundings and every thought that wasn't connected to the beautiful woman in his arms flew right out the window.

He was Adam and she was Eve. Nothing else existed in the world except the two of them together. For the first time in his life his feral nature and human soul were satisfied completely as one.

Jackson lost all of the doubt and confusion he buried so deeply about their relationship as if it had never been there. She wouldn't leave him. He knew she could never do that now. She was as much a part of him as he was of her and there was no way in the universe they could ever live separate lives.

The last thing in the world he wanted to do was pull away from her, but her shallow breathing beneath him indicated a need for oxygen. He rolled over on his back and she followed his movements, turning on her side as she slid her shapely thigh between his legs to rest up against him. Jackson shivered in delight to feel her smooth skin pressed next to his slick shaft as he began to grow aroused again.

He didn't know if she'd be ready to have him so soon, but after another minute of gentle caresses and nudges with her leg, he'd be forced to find out. He didn't think he could ever have enough of this beauty cradled in his arms and the sudden urge to kiss her enveloped him.

Jackson tipped her chin with strong fingers and claimed her lips with his hungry mouth. She responded to him instantly, parting his lips with her tongue and probing deeply. His desire ignited like a bonfire and he delved in for more.

He ran a strong hand along her curvaceous hip, his fingers pulling her close when he thought he tasted blood on her mouth.

A cold wave of horror shot through him and he abruptly disengaged himself from their embrace. Had he hurt her in some way? He thought he'd been gentle, but then there was a moment when he lost control. If he had done anything to injure her he didn't think he could live with the pain of it.

"Jackson?" her voice sounded drowsy, satiated, but he thought her speech seemed a bit sluggish.

He was filled with alarm as he reached for the lamp on the bedside table. His shoulder stung as his muscles stretched beneath the skin, but he paid it little mind in the midst of his concern.

She remained on her side where he rolled away, though she shielded her eyes with an upturned hand. He wasn't able to immediately identify any wounds on the exposed part of her body so he kneeled next to her for further inspection.

She had blood on the corners of her mouth. As he reached forward to remove her hand a stabbing pain shot through his entire upper body. He was used to pain, but this was something different.

A quick look at the mirror on her dresser behind them showed him a deep wound on his shoulder, blood still streaking over his taut muscles. It looked suspiciously like a bite mark and he turned again to his woman with the blood on her face.

"My God, Jessica! What have you done?" Jackson panicked, taking her wrist to count her pulse. His emotions were all over the place but his biggest fear, the one where he lost her, pushed to the forefront of his thoughts and his hands shook uncontrollably.

"I made a choice, Jackson." Her response was proud and strong. "For us to be together you had to live in my world, or I had to live in yours. You have a destiny with your family, my love. And in case you haven't noticed, my family is here now as well."

Did she do it for the love of him? Was it because Emily and Lucy were choosing to stay with the Hart clan, too? All those reasons were sound, except for the fact that she was risking her life to change.

"What if you can't turn? What if I lose you in the process?" He tried to keep his voice steady so she wouldn't be afraid. It was his job to be the one in control, yet she had taken all of that away from him in one night.

He had just found her and he didn't think he could survive losing her.

"I couldn't let you bear the burden of making that decision. But I have a secret, Jackson. One your mother gave me this very night before you came."

His mother! Damn that complicated woman and her intrigues. As much as he wanted to be angry with her at that moment, he fully knew now the terrible pain she must have experienced—still was experiencing—for the loss of his father.

"I don't care about secrets. I don't care about anything in this world except you. We have to get you down to the medical facilities right away." Jackson slipped an arm behind her back but she shrugged it away before he could pick her up.

"I'm not exactly at death's door, you know. I can walk just fine. But I want you to hear me out before we go any farther."

"You are the most vexing and difficult woman I have ever known!"

"Almost." She managed a smile. "Meredith told me the truth, Jackson. Your father never turned the two of you in that farmhouse. He decided he was going to use the formula on himself rather than compromise his lover and their son. Your mother is a strong woman and she realized his chance of surviving was much less than hers, and so she took the initiative. She bit him and turned herself."

"She told you this so you would risk your life instead of mine. She knew I would bond with you and nothing could stop me. In essence, she sacrificed you and I can never forgive her for that."

"Not necessarily. She felt the legend and lore surrounding the turning of humans was exaggerated. If you look around, you have to admit every person we know who has been bitten was turned, except for Lucy. And that's because the family doctor back home inadvertently did something to stop it."

"So, you're saying the risk of death from the change is not as grave as we'd been led to believe?" It had never occurred to Jackson before, but she certainly did have a point.

"Well, everything we do is a risk in life, I guess. But your mother believed the old world lore was more of a way to control the shifter population and maintain their secrecy than anything else."

"It doesn't matter to me, Jessica. I don't care if you have a ninety-nine-point-nine chance of surviving. I cannot and will never put you in harm's way."

This time she didn't protest when he helped her off the bed and put a steadying arm around her waist. He laughed a little when she modestly made sure her robe was tightly closed. Of all the things to worry about! She was his mate. Jessica could run naked through the manor waving pinwheels and no one would be fazed. His scent mingled with hers now and every other male in the household deferred to him.

He saw the small, nondescript package on the floor as they passed the door and easily reached down to pick it up. Whatever plans he had for it now didn't matter. Jessica had made the decision for them both and it would be best to keep the serum under lock and key once more.

•

Jessica was glad of Jackson's support as they approached the large foyer beyond the front door. Just when she thought everything might be alright she was alarmed to see a crowd gathered in the middle of the hall. There were a few raised voices and angry threats, all of which seemed out of character for the civilized Hart family.

Jackson motioned for Jessica to stay back and stalked to the outer ring of the mob. As soon as they noticed him they grew silent and parted to allow him access to the center. Jessica saw what everyone was so up in arms about, sprawled out on the floor and crying with her face in her hands.

A helpless girl! She was dressed in dirty rags and she couldn't have been more than seventeen if she was a day. Jackson's fists clenched in fury and waves of displeasure rolled off him as the crowd parted further. Soft, straight flaxen hair spilled over the young woman's fingers and as Jessica moved closer she raised clear, grey eyes to look at Jackson.

There was something familiar about the waif, though she couldn't place it. Her skin was almost white and covered in bruises, but the expression in her eyes struck Jessica the most.

"What is going on here?" Jackson turned in a semi-circle to look at the members of his clan. One brave male stepped forward and pointed a finger directly at the girl.

"She's one of the Dark Breed." His voice was full of anger as he glared at the small creature. She hunched over in response and growled menacingly at her accuser. It sounded so familiar, Jessica could nearly place it.

Wait! Is it even possible? Her mind raced as she closely examined the defensive figure on cold tiles. Jessica walked through the crowd at Jackson's back. Stepping to his side, she reached out a hand to the girl.

"What are you doing?" Jackson hissed in disbelief. She knew she was overstepping her bounds but she needed to get closer. The pale-faced urchin tilted her head to the side when Jessica drew near and relaxed her posture.

"Anna Lisa?" Her voice was shaky. It was a huge gamble, but if she was right she had to protect the girl. A look of recognition flashed across the terrified girl's face and in the blink of an eye she was on her feet with her arms wrapped around Jessica's waist.

Jackson sprung into action with a horrifying growl that chilled Jessica to the bone, but before he could place his hands on the child she encircled her shoulders defensively.

"Do you know her? How is that possible?"

She could see the rage in Jackson's eyes, the fear that this intruder had laid hands on her before he could react, but he still respected her enough to allow her actions.

"She saved me—and the ranger, too. On the day Roland took me to the cabin. She didn't back down when she could have abandoned us to the man and woman from the other pack."

"Anna Lisa?" She heard the smallest voice at the edge of the crowd. Sheriff Winters staggered through the outer mob, choking back a sob as he looked at the girl in disbelief. He held out his arms, openly crying while he waited for her to respond.

"Daddy?" The girl sounded confused for a moment, as if she was trying to remember another life.

Jessica released her, quickly blinking her eyes so she wouldn't cry in front of the family as Sheriff Winters fell to his knees. The ragged figure walked gracefully to her father and curled up on his lap. After he wrapped his arms around her shoulders he looked up at Jackson.

"You did it, Mr. Hart. I promised to keep your secret and you helped me find my daughter. I will never be able to thank you enough."

"You need to help them more, Daddy," she said quietly. Her words drew the attention of everyone in the room.

"What do you mean, Anna Lisa?" Jackson came close to the girl, doing his best to approach without startling her. Jessica followed, partly to hear what was going on, but also because she wanted to be at Jackson's side through all this.

"I came here to warn you." The teen's voice was angelic, her soft tones carrying innocence she knew the girl couldn't possess. "Something bad is going to happen soon. Bria and Justin have killed almost all of us. They told me I'd have nowhere to go, and if I went to Hart House the family would kill me."

There was a sad truth in the statement made by the renegade pack leaders. Who knows what might have happened if she and Jackson hadn't come along? At the end of the day, they were all animals.

"Tell me what it is, Anna Lisa. I promise you'll be safe from now on. You can stay here and we will always protect you. I owe you a huge debt of gratitude." Jackson's eyes flicked briefly over Jessica's form when he spoke.

"They're going to kill Michael at the farmhouse. After he turns himself human he'll be weak and won't be a match for them."

"What do you mean after he turns human? How is that possible?"

"I saw it. He took the vial and stuck a syringe in his arm."

"You must be mistaken, Anna Lisa." Jackson's voice was steady, but his knuckles were white as he produced the box. "I have the formula right here. He couldn't have used it."

She nodded to him and didn't dare to disagree, but Jessica could see the truth in her eyes. Jackson opened the lid and removed the padding inside the lined container to reveal the contents.

It was empty of everything except a picture in a wooden frame.

Chapter 22

"If this keeps up I'm going to need larger offices." Reginald said as he assisted Jessica onto the bed next to Lucy. Her recovering friend smiled when she saw her arrive, but a look of concern washed over her features when she realized Jessica was having her vitals read.

"What happened, Jess?" She tried to sit up on the narrow cot but the doctor was ready for her. He snapped his fingers as soon as she moved and David appeared out of nowhere to settle her back down.

"What hasn't happened would be a better question," Jessica answered cryptically.

She felt fine! All of this fuss was unnecessary. Anna Lisa required attention far more urgently than she did. Jessica could see her through an open doorway to another room, but Sheriff Winters hadn't let go of her yet and he sat right next to her on the examination table.

"This is all so crazy," Lucy whispered. "Every time I fall asleep I think I've been dreaming when I wake up. Then I see all of this."

"You're preaching to the choir there, sister. At least we get to be crazy together. We can wear matching hospital gowns at the psych ward and everything!"

Lucy managed to roll her eyes before her brows knitted together in confusion.

"Have you seen Michael, Jess? I can't remember a lot of what happened after he took me to the farm." This was the first time she had mentioned any memory of what occurred, but Jessica didn't think it looked like a painful recollection.

"Have I seen your evil werewolf boyfriend lately? No, sorry. My dance card has been full the past few days."

"Don't be like that, please Jessica." Tears sprang up in girl's eyes. "You love who you love. That's just the way it is."

"Hold still, young lady," the doctor warned her as he adjusted the blood pressure cuff on her other arm.

"I have to ask-" Lucy lowered her voice as far as it would go. "Did Jackson bite you, Jess?"

She heard the physician draw a sharp breath and all of a sudden she could have heard a pin drop in the room. He even stopped the blood pressure gauge where it tightened, which was uncomfortable to say the least.

"No, Lucy. He did not."

She thought she heard the doctor sigh in relief and the blood pressure cuff hissed in agreement as he released its hold. She rubbed her arm where the band had constricted before she turned back to Lucy.

"I bit him," she said simply.

A nearby tray containing a thermometer and various other medical implements went crashing to the floor with her admission. Reginald stood over the heap and the look on his face was a mixture of shock and displeasure. He bent down as soon as he caught her staring, but she could still hear him speaking low under his breath.

"Women in this day and age. What is the world coming to? The audacity of a woman initiating the process is inconceivable!" He stalked out of the room with the items from the tray in his hands.

"Next thing you know, we'll all be voting." Jessica barely suppressed a laugh, but Lucy straightened right up.

"And you think I'm reckless?" Her friend was clearly upset by the news. "What if you don't make it? I heard I was lucky to survive and from what I remember I was sick as a dog the whole time, too."

"No pun intended? But stop worrying over me. I'll be perfectly alright. I feel fine!"

•

"Jessica is fine. You and I both know it's far too early to tell if she's infected." The doctor delivered his report to Jackson with a solemn face, none of his displeasure over her circumstance showing.

He knew Reginald wouldn't approve that she was an outsider, or the manner in which it happened. He was prepared for that.

The elder male was a good friend to his late father and a valuable member of the Hart clan, but he was going to have Jessica at his side and that was the last word. Everyone was going to have to adjust.

"I realize it will take a little time to accept her into the family, Reginald. Your opinion on this is very important to me and I need your help if she's going to transition. You haven't gotten to know her as I have, but you'll see how amazing she is in due course."

"Don't get me wrong, Jackson." Reginald sighed heavily and sat down on one of the chairs in the study. "I find her to be an exceptional person. She is as lovely on the inside as she is on the outside. And so loyal to her friends! I can't remember the last time I encountered such a strong and capable woman. Perhaps since your father brought Meredith to me, in much the same way you did with Jessica."

"So, it's not that you disapprove?" Jackson carefully questioned the older man. He would be an important ally when it came to getting the rest of the family to accept his mate.

"I guess I'm just old fashioned – a romantic, you could say. Whoever heard of the woman taking the initiative? Really!"

"I trust you'll keep a close eye on her while I'm gone. Roland is gathering everyone to retrieve Michael from the old farmhouse immediately. We'll bring him straight to the ward when we get here, so be ready with anything you think you'll need."

"Jackson, you know there's a strong possibility Michael will not have survived the injection. And even then, what of the dangerous pair in his pack who betrayed him?"

"I don't want to hear that. I'm going to bring him back alive and well."

An unobtrusive knock on the study door shook him out of the unpleasant thought and he stood behind his desk, excusing the physician.

"She's not going to like that you left her behind again," Reginald said and Jackson nodded to him with a straight face. Perhaps the doctor was beginning to understand Jessica after all.

"I have no choice. Until we figure out if the bite has an effect on her she needs to stay close to home. Just make sure she remains in the vicinity of your office until I return."

"That's the first sensible set of instructions I've heard since she got here. I just hope I won't have to sedate her. Well, mostly." Reginald opened the door, revealing the gathering outside.

Jackson was surprised to see his mother among them, dressed for cold weather. He noticed she carried an extra down-filled coat and pair of gloves. One look in her eyes showed him the pain she had carried for so long was finally gone. She had kept her secrets with steadfast loyalty, but now that Jackson knew the truth a weight appeared to be lifted off her shoulders.

"Let's go get my son." Meredith stepped forward and put her hand on his shoulder. He was moved to see that almost every capable person on the house was marshaled and ready to fight for Michael and for the Hart name.

◆

The farmhouse looked abandoned as they approached. No smoke curled up through the chimney and no flickering flames lit the windows on the second floor. Somehow seeing the homestead empty filled Jackson with a sadness he couldn't readily define.

Several members of the rescue party circled around the edge of the clearing to approach from the back of the house. Sheriff Winters instructed the rest to scout the woods for any sign of the dangerous pair Anna Lisa and Jessica told them about.

Jackson experienced a moment of fear when he realized this might not necessarily be the place Michael would choose to sequester himself in his attempt to become human. He thought of the mural in the basement then, and how much it meant to his brother when he created it. He knew he couldn't be near Lucy when he took the formula so he would have stayed close to the next best thing.

"There doesn't appear to be any activity in the area." The sheriff's words reinforced his apprehension, but he still wouldn't allow himself to consider the fact that Michael wouldn't make it through this alive.

He motioned for the man to follow him. The rest of the party hung back as they stepped onto the porch. Nothing stopped them when they entered the front door, and Jackson was struck by how cold and run-down the place looked without the hearth lit. From the look of the ash in the grate, it had been quite some time since there was a fire.

The kitchen told the same story, but Jackson picked up a rustling noise through the open cellar door. The dank smell permeated the area, but there was no candlelight generated from below like before. A bit of feeble sunshine would be filtering through the dirty glass in the small windows, but not enough for Michael to paint by.

Sheriff Winters pulled a large flashlight from his belt and clicked it on. Jackson nodded in the direction of the stairwell leading down and the officer fell in line behind him.

Jackson took each step slowly, the hair on the back of his neck rising in warning as he remembered the stairway had no backing. He could hear the scuffle clearly now and thought it sounded like someone struggling.

He reached the bottom landing and turned to face Winters with relief when a hand darted from out of the shadows behind the steps. Before he could shout a warning the intruder grabbed the officer's ankle and sent him sprawling down the last few stairs at Jackson's feet.

The flashlight flew from the sheriff's hand and smacked against the wall. The beam spun wildly as it hit the ground, coming still to cast a solid ray of light on the slumped figure of Michael.

He was tied to a chair in the far corner of the cellar, held helpless near his mural. He was gagged and bound so completely it was a wonder he was able to strain against the trussing at all. His eyes were wide above the gag when he saw Jackson and he shook his head fervently.

"Oh good," a deep and ominous voice drawled with a southern accent from the darkness on the opposite end of the cellar. "Now we can have our little family reunion. And kill two birds with one stone, so to speak."

Jackson knew the voice must belong to Justin, but the reckless fool had given his position away with his verbal taunt. There was just one thing he needed to know before he put an end to all of this.

"We can't have a party without everyone present, now can we?" Jackson didn't turn his head toward the predator in the shadows. There was no sense in letting him know he was aware of his location if he didn't already.

"Where's your little girlfriend, Bria? I hear she likes the company of strong men so I'm sure she'll be interested in trading up. From everything Michael has told me, you're about as pathetic an example as they come."

Of course his brother hadn't told him that, but if Jackson could make him angry he'd be twice as likely to make a mistake. With any luck he'd come for Jackson instead of Michael, who couldn't defend himself.

He saw the sheriff crawl to his hands and knees in his peripheral vision, and he had the good sense not to retrieve his flashlight. Jackson could see several of the unused vials of serum nested on top of his mother's box of remaining journals, right where he prayed they would be.

"You're calling me pathetic?" The hidden assailant sounded too confident, his tone smug and it worried Jackson. "At least I didn't leave my women alone in a big old house with only an old man to guard them. Oh, I guess you did ask where Bria had gone, though, didn't you."

Justin's words tore through Jackson's body like knives when he realized the truth of his threat. Every fiber in his being became instantly alive with the need to protect his mate. He was shifting, unable to stop it as his primal instincts took over.

"Remember the plan!" he managed to shout to the sheriff, his voice turning gruff even as his body transformed before the old man's incredulous eyes.

Jackson's powerful muscles propelled him through the air and he landed directly on Justin's chest, knocking him senseless to the ground. Somewhere, deep within his animal rage, he knew the sheriff had a task to perform and it had to do with the prey beneath his heavy paws.

He hardly cared as his muzzle drew back to reveal his deadly, sharp teeth.

•

"I know it sounds completely ridiculous." Lucy sat on the edge of the bed inside the room she shared with Jessica in the medical ward. "When I first saw Michael at the Hocking Hills house I loved him completely. You don't believe in love at first sight, I know, but I swear that's what happened."

"You'd be surprised by what I believe in these days," Jessica said with open honesty. "But besides that … you're saying the biting and kidnapping and all that didn't scare you?"

"Oh Jess, it wasn't like that at all." A dreamy look took over her eyes and she actually smiled at the memory. "It was so sweet. He came to my window at the cabin and called to me. I wanted to open it, but it seemed like it was stuck. He broke the glass and reached inside to unlock it. He didn't even care that he cut himself at all. Then he told me how beautiful I was when I was sleeping and how he needed me to be near him."

"Oh, in that case I've judged him most unfairly," Jessica said. "I didn't know there was romance involved in your abduction."

"He's not the awful person everyone thinks he is, you know. He's spiritual and beautiful all the way through to his soul. He was just a little lost for a while. It happens to the best of us."

There was a time in Jessica's life when she never would have understood what Lucy was saying. With love, anything was possible. Even the impossible, apparently. The whole world felt different to her now and she found she could believe in anything, even a happy ending with Jackson.

She smiled to herself at the thought when the door to her room burst in, practically flying off the hinges as it crashed against the tile wall. She froze momentarily, but recovered her senses well enough to step in front of Lucy before Reginald's limp body was tossed through the open doorway onto the floor.

He landed heavily on top of the glass that shattered from the viewing window with a sickening thud. She knew from his grunt he was alive, but the amount of blood on his clothes was frightening. Bria entered the room crouched like a predator, the wicked crossbow Jessica had observed the day before at her side. Her black braids were pulled back in a pony tail and her eyes narrowed as she took in the room.

"You can stand in front of that bitch if you like, but I promise you I'll get around to you, too, before I'm through here."

Her black leather books crunched on the shards of glass as she stepped delicately over the still figure of the unconscious doctor. Jessica covertly looked around and found the only thing nearby she could use as a weapon—a sharp pair of scissors.

She grabbed the cold metal handle and shot forward as soon as her fingers made contact. She had always been taught to never pick up a weapon to defend herself unless she was willing to use it.

Bria's eyes widened when she saw Jessica meant business, and she raised her arm in front of her face. It deflected the blow only slightly because Jessica had momentum coming into the jab. The sharp point had grazed her scalp and blood trickled down over her right eye.

Jessica had just found out there really were such things as shape shifters and castles and prince charming. It was a whole new world and a new life. There was no way in hell this deviant was going to take it from her or Lucy as long as she had any breath left in her body.

She braced herself again, her fingers tightly gripping the scissors when she saw with alarm that Anna Lisa stepped into the door way behind Bria. She realized too late she had given the girl away with her reaction and pushed forward to distract the intruder. Unfortunately, Bria was ready this time and swung the cross bow high over her shoulder, bringing the butt down sharply on Jessica's head.

For a moment she just stood there, and then the cold tile floor tilted slowly until it laid itself against her cheek. She didn't feel any pain, but she couldn't move her limbs either. Bria turned on the young girl in the doorway a split second later, confident enough that Lucy was so weak she wouldn't be a threat.

"I'll deal with you last, moppet, because I like you best." The woman laughed a little maniacally before slugging Anna Lisa square in the jaw.

Jessica felt a whoosh of air on the back of her neck and she realized Lucy had dropped to the floor beside her. Her friend worked the scissors from her paralyzed fingers and she wanted to cry out for her to stop! Those would be what Bria used to kill her if she got hold of them.

The woman didn't waste much time with the young girl. She turned back to Lucy, who stepped in front of Jessica on the floor. Her hands were shaking behind her back, but Jessica could see the glinting metal she hid there.

"I suppose you think you're brave," Bria spat out. "I don't need this crossbow to kill you, so don't worry about that."

She let the wooden weapon clatter to the floor, still loaded with a barbed bolt.

"I hear all I need to do is bite you. You were weak as a human, and you're weaker now that you failed to change. I'll taste your blood and watch you die, just like your friends will before it's their turn."

"You better stop now, lady. I don't want to hurt you."

Jessica was surprised at the strength in Lucy's voice as she warned the advancing woman. A sneer twisted Bria's lips at the girl's bold threat and her eyes lit up with an eerie glow. A rustling sound came from the lobby of Reginald's office, but the woman didn't seem to hear it through her predatory lust.

A tiny growl erupted from the doorway, followed by a round of ferocious barking. Jessica managed to pull herself into a sitting position in time to see a small ball of fur come flying into the room, latching onto the fingers of Bria's right hand.

It was Scruffy! Jessica thought she'd never see her little protector again. She couldn't imagine what he must have gone through to get there and just in time to distract their attacker, too.

Bria swung him against the wall with a sickening thud, but he remained attached. Her howls of pain almost equaled the intensity of his growls through her bloody fingers. Lucy dropped to her knees at Bria's feet, taking no notice of the glass that cut into her delicate skin. With a quick flick of her wrist she opened the razor-sharp blades of the scissors and cut the tendons on both of Bria's ankles.

A look of shock crossed the intruder's face as the last member of the Dark Breed clan fell over, screaming and clutching the back of her heels. Lucy scampered back to Jessica to make sure they were both out of the flailing woman's reach.

Scruffy ran to them and Jessica was able to take him in her arms, though she didn't know if she was comforting the small dog or herself as she stroked his fur.

"Emily heard me talking to Granny on the phone about Scruffy." Lucy's voice wavered slightly as she spoke. "After I hung up she told me she'd have someone from the family find him and bring him back to us. It was going to be a surprise for you, Jess."

After everything they had been through, Jessica found it hard to believe the sight of her brave little dog was going to be the one thing to make her cry, but it happened. In an effort to control her emotions, she turned to Lucy who was closely examining the cut marks on her knees.

"How did you know to do that with the scissors, Lucy?"

"I went to nursing school for like six weeks, remember? Before I was a waitress but after the whole model thing went wrong." She didn't elaborate but Jessica knew exactly what she was talking about.

She vowed to never count her friend out for anything again. Lucy was always full of surprises and this one saved their lives.

She felt a little dizzy when she tried to stand, but was actually surprised by how quickly she had recovered from that nasty blow to the head. Just as Reginald pulled himself up to a sitting position, the massive form of a wolf hurdled over him in the doorway. He landed on top of Bria who was still whimpering in pain, and Jessica thought she heard the crack of bones and glass on impact.

Jessica recognized him this time as the wolf she saw off the back step at the ranger station. It was Jackson, and his raw, feral fury directed at the woman on the floor was awesome to behold.

"It's about time, old boy." Reginald rubbed his head where Bria had clubbed him as well. "Are we still following the plan?"

"There was a plan?" Jessica wasn't able to keep the incredulous tone out of her voice as she turned to look at the doctor.

"Believe it or not," Sheriff Winters answered, offering the older man a hand as he entered the room.

Both men walked over to where Jackson had the intruder pinned to the floor.

"This is nothing, I'll heal before you know it and then I'll come for you all!" She spat venomously at the doctor's feet, though he paid her repulsive actions no mind.

"I think not, my dear." The sheriff pulled out a small vial filled with red liquid. He carefully inserted a long needle and drew it out before he leaned down to insert it in her arm.

"No!" she screamed long and loud. "I'll tell everyone about you if you do this to me, they'll come looking for you all and finish what I started."

"We'll see. I already radioed ahead to the psychiatric ward at the hospital in Seattle to let them know you'll be coming. I highly recommended sedation, by the way."

"Is everyone else alright?" Jessica looked around quickly for Anna Lisa. The girl was already walking through the waiting room with a bottle of water in her hands. It had to be true, what their deranged attacker said before she was forced to submit. Their kind must heal very quickly.

But she didn't feel any different! Surely if something was going to happen to her she'd have noticed it by now? She remembered Lucy felt sick almost right away. Would Jackson still love her if she couldn't change? She looked to her mate who remained on top of the intruder beneath him

Bria struggled for a minute more under his massive weight and then drifted off as the effects of the formula began to work. Once the danger passed Jackson stepped away from her like she was nothing but rubbish and stood near Jessica. This was as close as she had ever come to any wild animal, let alone one as powerful and magnificent as a wolf.

She looked into his eyes and she saw Jackson there. She loved him with all of her heart, no matter his form. He truly was beautiful and she thought back to what Lucy said earlier about Michael. She realized Jackson's feelings would remain the same for her no matter what her condition was, because you love who you love.

"What of Bria's partner?" she asked the sheriff, almost feeling pity for the woman who had bonded with a man she would surely never see again. She understood how agonizing it would be to be separated from her mate.

"He got the same treatment he gave Michael after the injection rendered him vulnerable, and I can tell you he wasn't too happy about it. Once we used the formula on him he found out what it was like to be helpless, tied up at someone else's mercy. Though I dare say he was given a softer glove than he showed Michael when we had him transported off."

"So, they think he's crazy?"

"Wouldn't you?" He shrugged in a matter of fact way.

She wasn't able to answer that question. She still wasn't sure any of them weren't.

Epilogue

Jessica ran the back trails of the forest, alive and free. The crisp autumn air filled her lungs as she panted. She reveled at the beauty of nature in a way she had never done before. The dirt on the path was littered with fragrant pine needles. A handful of birds startled from within a nearby bush at her approach.

She longed to chase the graceful creatures as they took flight, landing safely in the lower limbs of a distant tree. But there was another distraction on the wind. The scents of fresh paint and turpentine assaulted her senses and she followed them to the source until she came upon a clearing.

Hanging back behind the tree line, she watched the human family for quite some time before she circled around for a better vantage point. She didn't make a sound as she stalked the small gathering. Their relaxed postures and laughter let her know they were none the wiser to her presence.

They spread out a blanket on the lawn and covered it with food and drinks. The scent of the fried chicken was tantalizing and her mouth watered. The parents of the small child held hands as they sat together on the blanket. They didn't seem to notice the toddler as he wandered in her direction.

Jessica faded back a little then, so he wouldn't catch her lurking there. It was no use and he stumbled across the lush, green grass, making a beeline for her spot. Finding himself in the cool shadows of the tall pines didn't seem to cow him as he stared through the trees.

Suddenly he laughed with delight and pointed straight at Jessica.

"Oh, you caught me!" She left her hiding place with her hands held up in surrender. She slipped on the slick needles as she emerged and twisted her ankle in the mud.

Great, there goes another pair of sneakers! She thought of all the shoes she's ruined one way or another in the forest.

"Mommy! Aunt Jessie here!" The boy ran off to the blanket and Lucy looked up to wave at her approach. Scruffy rolled over, sunning himself and he wagged his tail as she got closer.

"It's about time, too." Jackson came through the screen door of the old homestead with a pitcher of tea. He glanced with pride at the exterior of the farmhouse he and Michael were restoring together, before his gaze settled on her. "I am starving!"

"For food?" she smiled enticingly as she took the glass container from his hands, brushing her fingers over his briefly.

"Come closer." His deep voice rumbled under his breath as he snagged her waist to pull her close. "I hear there's a full moon tonight. Want to go for a real run with me later?"

"That depends," she whispered with a smile. "Do you think you can keep up?"

"Every day for the rest of your life, Mrs. Hart."

Jackson bent down to nuzzle her neck and the tiny hairs all over her body stood on end. She had almost mastered control of her transformations, but she still had a tendency to struggle in certain situations, mostly when she was aroused by her mate. Her husband knew this and delighted in tempting her whenever possible.

"Wait until after the picnic and then you can have your dessert." Her words were full of sensual promise and his eyes flashed with desire at her invitation. He truly had a delicious way of getting what he wanted from her, and giving it to him was the icing on the cake.

• • •

Kimberly Adkins

Kimberly Adkins resides in Ohio. She is an avid artist who works with oils, acrylics and water colors. She also spends time song writing and sometimes singing—but only when forced! She has always loved Egyptian lore, as well as science fiction and fantasy.

For Kimberly, writing romances is a wonderfully appealing outlet for "magic and passion."

KimberlyAdkins.com